THE WEBS SERIES

Imogene Nix

Love Books Publishing

GLOSSARY OF WORDS USED BY THE BA'TUAN

Da' This is a label akin to lady, given to a
woman who is considered worthy
(though may be bestowed on the mate of
a male given the title of De')
De' This is a label akin to lord, given to a
man who is considered worthy (though
may be bestowed on the mate of a
woman given the title of Da')
Deandara A term of endearment - similar to lover
Osphan A born noble who acts as bodyguard,
advisor and aide to a Turaa
Ti A generation of youngsters taught rigid
control over all emotions. (Though not
all have subscribed to this training)
Turaa Prince
Turana Princess

ISBN 9781922369406

BOOK ONE: FATED WEBS

Earth of 2030 supports a colony of Ba'Tuan — the men and women came to Earth in the hopes they'll learn to overcome the rigid control of the *Ti* generation.

Valerie is an ordinary earth woman, living an ordinary life. At thirty—four, her daughter Gia is now a young adult and Valerie's content with her world. That is, until she meets Joruzan. He's sexy, smart and makes her feel things she's sure she's too old to feel.

But Joruzan is just as determined to prove her wrong and get the woman he's fated to love.

Chapter 1

The world stood still. Every television station blared the same story and the same scenes.

They plastered the internet and print media.

Aliens from space make contact.

Valerie Montgomery was caught up in the mix of excitement and fear, just like every other human.

Her daughter, Gia ignored the news though, as she completed her homework on the mat in front of Valerie's desk.

Unlike so many others Valerie couldn't take the time away from her burgeoning business, so instead, she'd brought the small television into her office.

"Mum? Why is aliens coming to Earth so important?" Gia was only six and not yet aware of the changes this could potentially bring to humanity. Or the danger.

She dragged in an unsteady breath. "Because with this, everything changes, Gia. Now finish your homework while I get this website updated. Then we'll go make dinner."

Still, though she should be working, Valerie's eyes strayed once more to the television.

Everything will change. Whether for good or bad, no one yet knew.

⁂

*V*alerie sighed, rubbed her aching feet and scurried down the sidewalk, more than a little aware that she was on a time limit. Get to the bank. Plead the case for an overdraft.

A tingle at the back of her neck had her stopping. She turned. Gaped.

There on the corner she spied them. Dressed in the clothing she'd only seen on the television. The Ba'Tuan's. Striding toward her.

"Excuse me, ma'am. You need to move." A man in black, earpiece dangling by a curled cord waved at her.

"Oh, yes." Embarrassment scorched her cheeks and she stumbled, nearly fell. A hand reached out to steady her.

"You are unharmed?"

The oddness of the query had her glancing up into the most beautiful eyes she'd ever seen. "I... Uh, yeah." She raised a hand, meaning only to smooth back a curl which dropped over her face and the man in black captured her arm, squeezing hard. "Ouch!"

"She means no harm, Mr Buetel. You can release her." The voice smoothed over her mind. Settling the nerves that suddenly warned her of danger.

"But she..."

"All is well. She merely dropped her papers."

Valerie glanced down and groaned as they flapped in the tiny breeze. She bent to scoop them up and the man beside her, the *Ba'Tuan* dropped to a knee to assist. "I'm sorry," she muttered feeling an unfamiliar sense of disconnection.

"It's is fine, lady. I will assist."

He did exactly that, then handed her the papers once they'd been collected.

A sound echoed, the bong of a clock in the distance. It cleared the veil settling over her mind. "Oh, no!" She stepped back. "Thank you but I have to go!"

Now, she turned and scurried up the road, refusing to give in to the urge to glance over her shoulder once again.

Chapter 2

Twelve Years Later

"Hey mum!" Gia's voice floated through the office. It wasn't a big space. Not really. They'd moved into the warehouse some four years ago when it became obvious to Valerie that to expand meant hiring an assistant and investing in more stock.

The house were they'd live wasn't big enough to contain the stock she held on hand.

"What?"

Gia rounded the corner and not for the first time, Valerie was amazed that the beautiful young woman she's given birth to was an adult.

"You have a request. From the *Ba'Tuan* High Commission."

Valerie sat upright. Startled. "Who?"

Gia grinned. "The *Ba'Tuan* High Commission. They want to talk to you about the line of art pieces you'd commissioned from Francisco's Co-op."

Valerie blinked. "The paper craft images?"

"Yep. They want to meet with you next week. I spoke with Sandra to ensure we can supply them."

Amazement didn't come even close to explaining her reaction to the request. Francisco's work was dramatic and lifelike. Created from recycled papers. Beautiful... But was it enough to attract the notoriously straight-laced *Ba'Tuan's*?

Sandra popped her head around the door. "They want to talk to you about importing the line... We'd have to discuss this with Francisco. See if his people can commit to the numbers their talking about. This could be good news though, for Montgomery Industries. You could grow the business. Take on more staff."

Glancing at Sandra, Valerie knew the woman was only stating the truth. Montgomery had to grow and soon, otherwise it would stagnate. Her assistant had been raising the concerns for the last year. Even worse, Valerie knew everything she said was correct and had been looking for ways to make the necessary changes and take an educated chance.

With a sigh, she laid down the report she'd been checking when Gia entered the room. "Yes, we should make an appointment. Sandra? Talk to Francisco, see what his people can manage. Gia? We need a proposal. Costings and overheads for us. Fees for exporting so we can look at a possible cost structure. We need to make enough that we can pay for another staff member."

Gia grinned. "Well, I'd love to be paid."

Valerie rolled her eyes. "You would be better getting a degree and working outside the business Gia. Gain some experience so when you do come back to Montgomery you'll have a well rounded experience of the business world."

It wasn't that she didn't want her daughter working for her. She was clever, bright and had an eye for detail, but truthfully, Valerie still feared that one day the business would fail. She wanted Gia to have something to fall back on.

Gia growled. "I'd rather work for you."

"I know, my love. One day."

Chapter 3

One week later

Valerie Montgomery looked at the pile of papers that littered her desk. "Some days I don't know if this business is worth it."

Sandra, her assistant snickered. "I'm glad you get to deal with that, and not me."

Of course, Sandra didn't know the half of it. The *Ba'Tua Turaa*, Cedun, was due to meet with her and she desperately needed to clear her desk, before he arrived. The problem was, where the hell was she supposed to even put it all?

Montgomery Industries was in trouble, and unless he allowed her to export to their homeworld, she'd be bust before the year was out. A truth she'd only come to realise in the last few days. Their stock was limited, the bank wanted a surety she couldn't give and the accounts were near to empty.

The need to look at least semi-successful rode her hard.

"Sandra, help me move them all to the break room. I don't want him to think we're incapable of dealing with..." She waved her arms over the scattered papers.

"Sure. I'll do this. You get the rest of the stuff in place."

Stuff being the drinks and choice canapés she'd organised. Her research had pointed to that being an integral part of the bargaining process.

As she laid them out, the hammering came at the door. She bit her lip hard, her tooth slicing through the soft flesh of her lip. "Ouch! Sandra?" Her attention splintered. She gripped the knife and the edge slid through her skin. "Damn!"

"Yeah, I'll get it!"

Thudding steps and the sound of the door opening wide had her senses jittering.

"Oh! Umm, it's Gia, Valerie. Do you want...?"

"What?" The word slipped out before she could contain it, and her daughter, sauntered in.

"Valerie? What's up? Hey, you've hurt yourself." Gia rushed in and grabbed her hand. "How the hell did you do that?" The ripping sound of tissues being dragged from their box filled the air. "Here, press that in place. I came over hoping there was some way I could help."

Valerie and Gia looked so similar, that many times they'd been taken for sisters. Valerie dabbed at the blood as she watched her adult daughter right the mess on her desk. Born when Valerie was only sixteen, she'd been the constant that held her together over the long years. Now, here she was as an adult, helping her out. Tears pricked her eyes burning her.

"Don't cry. It'll all be okay." Gia pressed a quick hard hug to her and dug out the proposal's she'd printed for Valerie. "I can stay if you need me?"

Valerie thought for a moment then shook her head. "No, I'll be fine once I've finally met the *Ba'Tua*."

Gia nodded. "Okay. But only if you're sure?"

Valerie smiled, hoping she was hiding the hornets nest of nerves that flew in her stomach. "It's fine. You go on home."

Gia left and Valerie slumped into her seat. "I only hope I haven't bitten off more than I can chew."

⁜

*J*oruzan wasn't totally sure why Cedun had demanded his presence at the meeting with himself and the owner of Montgomery Industries.

"Come. This is the appointed time." Cedun indicated the door and Joruzan followed him inside.

The woman sitting at the desk flashed them both a welcoming smile. "*Turaa*. We are honoured…"

"It is *our* honour. This is Joruzan, my…assistant, but please, call me Cedun."

Joruzan contained the mild irritation at Cedun's strange title for him. He was really more than an assistant, but humans seemed to struggle with the concept of *Turaa's Osphan*, the exact title he owned.

Joruzan was a noble in his own right, he also acted as Aide, Chief Bodyguard and even Advisor to the *Turaa*, or prince, when they were far from home. Like now.

"Of course, please come this way." The woman waved them to a small office and opened the door. "Uh, Valerie Montgomery."

His mind blanked settling on the woman. His body instantly reacted to her, hardening with the force of instant desire. Just as it had all those years ago on the roadside. He remembered the blush staining her cheeks, the scent of her body. He had to supress the emotions churning inside him. "De' Valerie." He extended his hand, as did Cedun and only dimly noted that she reciprocated with himself and Cedun.

His body was still absorbing the knowledge of the shock that rippled through his system. *My mate.*

"Uh, as you would be aware, we've made representations to export to your homeworld but…"

Cedun leaned back in his seat as Joruzan watched the play of concern on De'Valerie's face.

"You have prepared a proposal, you stated." Cedun's voice cut through the fog and Joruzan sat upright. *I'm here to advise Cedun, not wallow in the knowledge that I've finally found my other half.*

"Uh. Yes, I have." Two small folders were pushed over the desk and Joruzan scooped one up and started flicking through, hoping to hide the sense of urgency that built within him.

De'Valerie's gaze settled on his and he detected a surge of pink. *She's embarrassed? Why?*

The meeting progressed slowly while Joruzan fought to keep his mind on the discussion. The canapés were delicious, he was sure, but he didn't really taste them.

He glanced at a photo behind her, of herself and a younger woman. "Your sister?" He pointed and De' Valerie blushed deeper.

"My daughter."

Hope plummeted. *Daughter.* Partner. Not for him.

"You are..." The word *mated* stuck in his throat but she shook her head.

"No, it's just me and Gia."

⁂

*V*alerie heaved a sigh of relief when the *Ba'Tua* left. "Well, that's it. I hope the proposal is enough to sway them."

"Me too. Mind you, they're both really good looking, aren't they?" Sandra chirped and Valerie smiled.

You go on home and I'll clear away and close up. Thanks for everything."

But once Sandra had left, she dropped back down into her seat. Oh, they'd been good looking all right, but they were Ba'Tuan's of the *Ti* generation. Sent here to learn to loosen their control.

Cedun was lovely, friendly and helpful but Joruzan... Now he fired her blood as no one else ever had.

Her body had reacted in a totally unfamiliar way, warming through and she'd felt this odd kind of emptiness deep down in her abdomen.

"You're too old for that kind of nonsense."

The door to her office swung open. "Everything is right, De'Valerie?"

There he stood, Joruzan. The sexiest man, to her mind, in the entire galaxy.

He was tall and muscular with black hair and golden eyes, that reminded her of pools of molten caramel. Her insides melted a little further.

"What kind of nonsense, De' Valerie?" His eyes gazed deep and she was nearly lost.

"I... Uh..." He flowed around the desk to stand before her. "I... Did you forget something?" The words came out like a throaty whisper and she blushed. Deeply.

Oh great work, Valerie. He probably thinks your some sex crazy middle-aged cougar wanna-be!

"I left my transmitter behind." But his gaze wasn't on her desk. No, it had settled on her face, or more specifically her lips.

She licked them, as they'd become dry then was aware of her actions. The blush deepened.

"Beautiful De' Valerie." Somehow, she missed that he'd moved even closer, so that with a single sway she could touch her body to his. He reached out and cupped her shoulder and she gulped.

"Uh..."

"*Deandara.*" The word caressed her mind and she sucked in an unsteady breath as he inched closer and pressed his lips against hers.

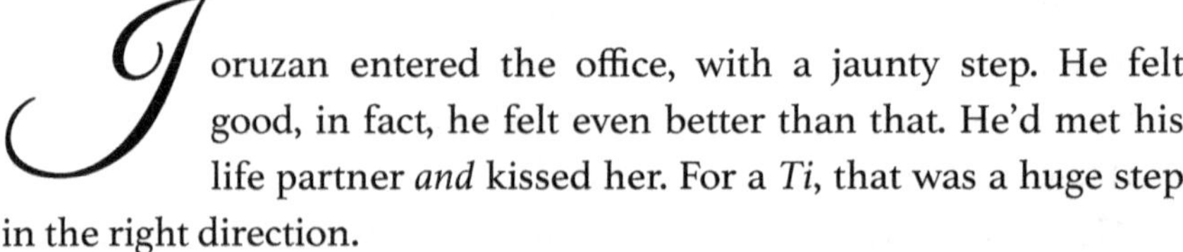

*J*oruzan entered the office, with a jaunty step. He felt good, in fact, he felt even better than that. He'd met his life partner *and* kissed her. For a *Ti*, that was a huge step in the right direction.

Even better, she hadn't shied away from him because he was *Ba'Tuan.*

Thinking back to Valerie, a vision of her rose. Her pale green eyes, and raven coloured hair with lush curves and ivory skin.

"You are happy? What happened?" Cedun waited by the window, his eyes narrowed.

"I've found my *partner*. De' Valerie."

Cedun staggered a little, then pushed away from the desk. "Then I congratulate you." There was an air of something wrong about Cedun and Joruzan stepped toward his friend.

"But all is not well for you?"

Cedun waved away his concern, but there was a distance opening between them, confusing Joruzan. "Cedun? *Turaa*?"

"It is nothing. Come, let us discuss this proposal. Does it have merit? You inspected it from cover to cover while in the meeting."

There was nothing more he could do but deep in his gut, he knew there was a problem that Cedun was refusing to discuss with him. *I will wait until he's ready.*

"I do. Her business is small, but these are handmade articles that she sells. Each is a work of art in its own right, that she sources from the artisan. She's offering us first rights on the stock."

"You feel this is right? That she can continue to stock our needs?" Cedun's tones were low and Joruzan didn't know quite what to make of his odd behaviour, then shook his head. Who knew with the *Ti*. They all carried odd baggage from the *Ba'Tuan* upbringing.

Joruzan squinted. "You won't tell me what causes you this issue? You are not happy with Montgomery Industries?"

"No. It's not that. Just... Place the order in the morning, Joruzan. We'll trial her wares."

⁂

*V*alerie spent an, tossing and turning. Memories of that kiss kept rolling through her mind. Joruzan, a Ba'Tuan had kissed her. Her mind had turned to mush and even now, the memory alone, made her knees weak and jellylike.

"Hey Mum! I've got an interview later today for a full-time job, but

I'll be in to help with the stocktake this morning, if that's okay?" They'd long ago agreed that in the workplace she'd use her mothers name but at home she'd still be mum.

Valerie dragged her distracted mind back to Gia. "Sure, that's great news." She shoved the spoon into the cold cereal and started when it clattered. Looking down, she realised the bowl was empty and Gia was giving her one of her *what's on your mind* looks.

"We should go." She shoved away from the table, grabbing the bowl and pushed it into the sink. Gia rose and followed suit, then picked up her bag and folder and together they headed out the door. Only as she climbed into the car did she realise it was barely seven a.m. and much earlier than they'd usually get on the road. She'd forgotten to even clean her teeth.

Wisely, Gia stayed silent on whatever she thought.

At the warehouse-come-office, Gia and Valerie unlocked the doors and started laying out stock. They weren't direct to the public, but sometimes the odd sale happened at the office door and Valerie never argued. Money was money, to her mind, remembering the times she and Gia had gone without over the years.

By the time eight a.m. crawled around, she was in front of her computer, sipping on a strong coffee.

When the door opened she started. Joruzan. Even his name sent tremors of excitement coursing. He was followed by the *Turaa*, Cedun, who had a totally shell-shocked look on his face.

"De' Valerie, we came to place an order." Joruzan spoke softly and she smiled.

"I'm so glad! I uh... That's wonderful. Here sit down and be comfortable." Just as she was urging the Turaa to take a seat the door opened and Gia entered the office.

"Valerie, I have..." She broke off and looked in her direction. "Oh... Uhhh, sorry."

Gia blinked owlishly at Valerie's arms on the Turaa.

"Oh... Cedun, this is my daughter, Gia." She indicated in Gia's direction and saw the faintest glint in Cedun's eyes and understanding hit. *He's interested in my daughter? She's too young!*

When her gaze collided with Joruzan's there was more than a thread of amusement and she blushed. *And I've got a crush on Joruzan. Oh my God! And I'm too old for this kind of nonsense.*

Gia tried to withdraw but Cedun and Joruzan wouldn't allow that.

"The Ba'Tuan's wish to place an order."

"Oh... Really? That's so exciting. Do you think... Uh..."

Cedun smiled at Gia and for a moment Valerie wondered if he was about to ask her out. Then the smile died away. "Cedun and Joruzan."

"Oh great. Umm, Turaa Cedun, maybe we could get a photo? I like to make sure Valerie has all kinds of memories of these kinds of events." Gia indicated to the walls and Cedun smiled.

"Of course." Naturally Cedun took the middle position between the women and Joruzan took to the photo, then she settled in and participated in the order preparation. They hadn't been at it long when Gia rose with a startled cry.

"Ohmygosh! Is that the time? I've got an interview." She spun shooting a horrified look in Valerie's direction.

"Take my car." Valerie passed her the keys and Gia ran out the door.

"That's quite a young woman, you have there." Cedun's voice was full of interest and she turned to him.

"She is. She's very special."

When Joruzan spoke though, he shocked her even more. "She's almost as special as her mother."

Chapter 4

*J*oruzan waited, though it felt like his guts were being wrung, until three days later.

Don't appear too impatient the human men insist. Not if you're interested in her as a woman.

How can I not be? It wasn't just the beauty and the poise of Da'Valerie that appealed. There was a softness many women of the earth appeared to have thrown off in the process of 'finding themselves.' The term he found contradictory, for where they not exactly where they were meant to be?

Trepidation slid through his veins. He might be Ba'Tuan but unlike many of the Ti generation, he'd not learned to control his desires. It was Da'Valerie that he truly desired. Not just the woman but as his destined mate.

There was an instinct, according to the old learnings that came with exposure to their mate. All they had to do was listen. But the Ti? They controlled themselves rigidly. Too rigidly to understand the learnings. For most of the Ti, taking a mate was a matter of a transaction. The physical interactions required to complete the conception unemotional and cold.

"You have made contact yet?" Cedun enquired.

Joruzan who'd been staring at the communications device grimaced. "Not yet, *Turaa*."

"Ring her, friend." The words were soft, closing the distance between the two men.

"What if she finds me..." he searched for an adequate word to describe what she might react with, "repugnant?"

"Then she is not meant for you, Joruzan." Cedun's quiet words didn't dispel his concerns.

He heard the footsteps and turned. Cedun loomed close. "We are not like the majority of the Ti, Joruzan. We feel. We want. We desire."

"And we hurt," he mumbled.

"Yes, we do. But if we don't take the chance, we will never know. Your fear *controls* you."

Cedun couldn't have used a more calculated term. He reached out and lifted the hand piece. Dialled the number.

"Montgomery Industries, this is Valerie."

He gulped. "Da'Valerie, I would like to ask if you'd join me, for lunch?"

⁘

*V*alerie fluffed her hair, glancing at her make up and wondering for the fiftieth time if it wasn't too much. Was she too... *anything*?

Gia entered the room and stopped three steps away. "Mu... Valerie?"

Spinning, Valerie felt awkward and silly. "I... I have a lunch with Joruzan."

"The Ba'Tuan?" Gia's voice rose.

"Yes."

"To discuss the deal?" Gia's eyes narrowed.

"I imagine so, Gia. I mean why else—"

Gia sighed, a wealth of frustration filling the sound. "You're so dense sometimes, Valerie. He was practically *eating you* with his eyes."

A blush stung her cheeks. "Nonsense!"

Gia strode forward, grabbed Valerie by the shoulders and spun her. "You're only just in your thirties. You're beautiful, clever and witty. You own and run a business you created by yourself. Any man would be pleased to have you."

Valerie bit her lip. "But I have an adult daughter."

"Listen, I may be eighteen, but lots of women your age are just finding their husbands. They're getting out there, having fun. Living their lives. You had me young, so what? I'm not like a wart on your nose."

"No. But you're my first concern."

"Bullshit. You're scared, but at my age you'd already started building Montgomery. You had a two year old. You were like an old settled woman before you could finish school. Now is your chance. Take it. Use both hands."

Fear coursed. "But what if..."

"What if's don't count in life. Just like you've always told me."

"But I'm thirty-four, Gia."

"You're also a woman. Now stop complaining and let's get you ready for your date."

"He didn't call it a date."

Gia simply smiled. "More fool him, then. I got this fabulous dress this morning on special, but it'll look better on you, I think." With that Gia dragged her into the tiny break room and set about preparing her for lunch.

Chapter 5

*J*oruzan's nerves were tight as he waited for Valerie to arrive, his hand laying on the white table cloth, his gaze scanning until suddenly she was there.

Her raven hair a wave of loose curls, her svelte body outlined with a dark blue dress but it was the uncertainty in his eyes that called to him. He rose, having observed the ways of human men since their arrival on earth several years ago.

"Uh, Joruzan. Hi." Her voice held a breathless quality.

He smiled. "Welcome *Deandara*. Please, take a seat."

Only when she'd perched on the edge of her seat did he lower himself back to his own.

The waiter came and slid menus before them both and hovered nearby as they made their selections, not that he could have cared what they dined upon for he was filling his vision with her. Finally, satisfied the waiter melted away and he watched as the tension filled Valerie's features.

"Uh, so Joruzan. You wanted to meet?"

"I did, Valerie. I wish to know you. Know more of you and your life."

Her eyes opened wide as did her mouth. "I... I'm flattered but—"

Confusion filled him. "You do not wish to know me too? I am not of interest?"

Understanding flashed on her face. "You... You are..." Valerie cleared her throat. "You're interested in *me*?"

Such surprised put paid to the emotions that warred deep inside him. "I do wish to know you Valerie. Within me I feel such things as most *Ti* will never understand. I would know you, and if in time we both agree, I want... more."

Heat suffused her. A flock of butterflies took up position in her belly if the quivering was anything to go by. All the more potent was the fact that she too felt that drawing. The hunger to be close enough that she might touch him.

Confusion warred deep inside though, excitement tempered by the knowledge she was a single mother, on the verge of being middle-aged. *Why? Why does he find me of interest?*

⁂

*V*alerie's head spun by the time he squired her home. An old fashioned word, she knew, but the most correct to explain how he'd made her feel.

Special.

Desired.

She hadn't felt those emotions in such a long time.

The door opened before she could slide the key in the lock. Gia's gazed settled on her face and surely, she must be able to see the change? The subtle swelling of her lips from Joruzan's kisses?

"So?" There was a wealth imbuing the single word question.

"He wishes to court me."

Gia's eyes widened. "Court you?"

Valerie slid her handbag to the table. "That's what he says. I told him I need time. He's willing to give me that. But I feel..." *How do I tell my almost fully grown daughter that I feel such desires? That my body desires sex and my heart the kind of companionship I've never really experienced?*

"So, do I need to have the birds and bees talk with you?"

Valerie choked. "What?"

"You know. Safe sex. Not getting pregnant. The kind of thing." Gia's eyes lit with naughty humour yet Valerie detected concern too. Her heart filled with pleasure that her daughter cared enough to be worried.

"I'm not looking to rush anything, Gia. I need time. After all, he's *Ba'Tuan* and I'm human. We don't even know if it's possible for me to get pregnant or even have sex with him."

"Uh, the sex bit *is* possible."

Valerie straightened up, as fury filled her. "Who was it? I'll—"

"Not me, Mum. I was watching one of those shows on television. You know, with the panels. Apparently they can be very very good. As lovers."

Now Valerie coloured. Heat washing off her. "You... Okay, let's organize dinner."

"So you can avoid the conversation?"

"Something like that, Gia," she countered and rose.

Chapter 6

*J*oruzan tidied his small house, frustration and concern filling him. After months of careful woo'ing, De' Valerie had agreed to a dinner date here. At his home. The *Ti* didn't usually participate in the local customs, but for Valerie, he'd do anything. He just hoped she'd accept what he planned to offer her tonight.

The buzzer sounded and he pushed the door open. Valerie stood in the doorway, clearly uncomfortable.

He ushered her in, his nostrils filling with the light floral scent she preferred.

"Oh Joruzan, what am I—?"

Unable to help himself, he swept her up in his arms and placed his lips to hers. His body a tight mass of need, that ached day and night for the completion he knew he'd only find with her.

They both moaned as desire bloomed. Eventually, he pulled away, noting they were both breathing heavily and a hectic colour high-lighted her cheeks.

"*Deandara...*" He reached out with a gentle hand and pushed away a lock, so it lay behind her ear. "I've waited a long time."

"But Joruzan, I'm old and..."

He placed a gentle finger against her soft lips. "No, *Deandara*. You are perfect to me. In every way."

"But..."

"*Deandara*, trust me. You are my partner. The love I've waited a long time to find. Believe in me and the emotions that we share. The *Ti...* Most don't feel deeply. Those of us who have not bound our instincts and needs? Once we find our mate, then no matter how well we are trained i nothing can quell our desire and need. Both to protect and be with our other half. That is what you are to me."

"I... But I have a grown up daughter. I can't... How can you claim to have me as a mate? I mean—" His gut ached at the distress on her face.

"*Deandara*, trust me and trust in us."

He watched as she wrestled with her emotions, before she cast him a tremulous smile. "I... Yes. I do."

Joruzan held out his arms and she walked into them and when he closed them around her, he'd never felt so complete.

"She thinks... Gia thinks I'm going out with Cedun."

He grunted, well aware of what her daughter thought. Joruzan had only met her once, but Cedun regularly updated him. Cedun having stepped up after Joruzan had declared Valerie as his mate to undertaken any business affairs. It meant that when Joruzan and Valerie were together they could learn about each other and grow the connection between them.

Not that Gia knew better. After the first outing with Joruzan, Valerie had explained Gia had found a boyfriend and quickly moved in with him. Valerie's spending time with Cedun, she'd taken to mean that Valerie had moved on and they'd formed an attachment. On one level that worried and angered him, but Valerie had insisted they leave her thinking that for now.

It had taken time for Joruzan to understand why Cedun spent so much time at Valerie's warehouse too. Then it clicked into focus.

"Cedun feels for your daughter."

"I know. But he won't let me tell her anything right now. It's odd..."

"Because of Da' Garret? There's something wrong there."

"Oh I agree, Joruzan, but I think he's still seeing other women, even though he's now with Gia."

"I should talk to him."

Valerie stepped back and framed his face with her hands. "She's too grown up for that. It would smack of interference and I... It just wouldn't be right. We'll just give it time, it'll sort itself out. I hope."

He growled in the back of his throat. Because it pained Valerie, it angered him.

"Joruzan?" Her thumbs rested on his cheek and he turned his head to plant a kiss on her hand.

"I love you, Valerie. I want to be with you in every way, until I am no more."

She gasped and her eyes opened wide. "I thought... "

He loved the way she blushed like a young girl. "I don't understand how you can possibly feel that way about me, but I... I feel the same. I love you too, Joruzan."

"Good."

"But..." She slipped her fingers against his lips stilling his actions. "We'll need to tell Gia. *Soon.*"

"Of course, *Deandara*. When you're ready, we shall disclose all. Now then, we should carry on with our plans for the evening, yes?" He sealed their agreement with a kiss which led to more. Much more and eminently satisfying. For both of them.

BOOK TWO: TANGLED WEBS

In the course of a single day Gia Montgomery loses her job and discovers that her boyfriend—now ex-boyfriend—is a two-timing sleaze. After downing a bottle of wine, she catches sight of Cedun, the *Ba'Tua* heir who has been living on Earth for several years, in her backyard. Gia's struggled to ignore the strong attraction between them, because she's sure he's seeing someone else. Someone very close to her, in fact.

When the situation with her ex turns nasty, Cedun finally has a chance to set things straight between himself and Gia, but nothing is as simple as it seems. Cedun must protect Gia and sort out an impossible love-life tangle before it's too late.

Warning: This title contains sexy aliens and feisty heroines, together with enough action—of every kind—to keep readers on the edge of their seats.

CHAPTER 1

Gia slumped down onto the wooden tabletop. "I hate my life."

Since this morning her carefully ordered world had fallen down around her. She'd overslept, missed the train, and arrived at work two hours late.

If that wasn't bad enough, Jeffrey, her boss, had called her into the office and told her, "Gia, I have some bad news. The company is shutting its doors."

Losing her job was certainly a biggie. But when she arrived at Garret's—early, due to the shut-down—Garret, her lover, had been home...with chesty bimbo 'Floss'. Gia had thought only to surprise him, maybe even soak up some sympathy, but when she let herself into his apartment she had found them in bed. Naked. Rolling around like overactive, loud teenagers.

It was a sight she wouldn't forget in a hurry.

The bottle clanked beside her head as she moved her hand. It tipped and the dregs of wine splashed their way across the tabletop. "Shit!"

She reached for the tissue box and mopped up the mess. Hunting for the rubbish bin, soggy tissues in hand, she jumped when the phone rang. Gia waited, wondering what more depressing news she could possibly receive.

Hi, this is Gia. I'm not available to take your call, so leave a message.

"Gia? This is Valerie. I heard about your job—and Garret. Call me."

Gia groaned. *Oh, why is life so unkind?* Her mum, Valerie, wasn't the nurturing, baking biscuits kind of mother. No, instead she was more like a friend. A close and tight friend.

"Right now a traditional parenting arrangement would be infinitely welcome." She glanced around, thankful that no one would hear her say that.

With several wobbly steps, she thrust the used paper into the bin and moved to the sink, gripping it firmly.

Nothing had been the same since the *Ba'Tua* had made contact with Earth. Now hospitals had shut down. The advanced healing techniques had been made available to all with tremendous success, putting traditional medical attendants out of work. Of course, the same was the case for many industrial outlets too. Including her place of work.

"So much has changed in the last three years." Her voice echoed in the empty kitchen as she gazed blindly out the window.

Earth now had several trading partners off-planet and long-term issues, such as global warming, had been eliminated with the help of the *Ba'Tua*.

But there was a catch. The *Ba'Tua* needed to learn to break free of the restraints they'd learned as younglings—so they could procreate and learn to live as one society. So groups were sent to settle on Earth. To learn to be *free*.

The *Ba'Tua* had been technologically advanced but hideously repressed, with a look-but-don't-touch attitude to life. The generation of '*Ti*'—the ones who'd made first contact—could barely handle being close to one another. They might be technologically advanced but their social skills, for the most part, were sadly lacking. Especially those who'd just arrived.

She snickered. "Must make sex a difficult prospect." Not that the

Ba'Tua discussed that either.

Of course, Earth wasn't the only planet they'd been working with, but to date, it seemed to have been the most successful species they'd encountered in terms of helping them overcome their issues. Just this morning, she'd seen several younglings, as the children were known, on the train, laughing and flirting with a group of girls.

For a moment a smile curved her lips. *Shame the men are so damned sexy.* The women weren't hard on the eyes either, Gia conceded.

Turning away from her position, Gia caught sight of movement from the corner of her eye. This time she looked out the window and in her garden was a *Ba'Tua* male.

"Holy hell, what's *he* doing here?"

Gia headed for the door just as Cedun was removing his Montgomery Industries t-shirt by the side of the pool. Her mind was sluggish and her coordination impaired, and she slammed into the edge of the door as she scurried through it.

"Shit!" The curse escaped her mouth as she kept moving, her hand rubbing the injured section of her side. "Cedun, what the hell are you doing in my backyard?" In her haste, she didn't see the hose on the deck and tripped.

She did notice the bright violet of his eyes—wide and startled— and the bronzed rippling muscles as she cartwheeled, flailing for something to grab onto, then she was falling backward. *It's all so slow!* A *thunk* sound married with the explosion of pain in her head.

The water closed around her and invaded her mouth and lungs. Her chest burned as the water weighed her down. Just as it all seemed too much, strong, vise-like arms slid around her middle, hauling her up to the surface.

"Do not struggle, Gia. Let me help you." He did, hauling her out of the pool and laying her flat on the concrete.

Then he rolled her over as she hacked and coughed. Water gushed from her mouth and nose, and she moaned once the indignity was over.

"Now, De' Gia, tell me why you ran out of the house and threw yourself into the pool. De' Valerie told me that you had been removed from your post. It cannot be that which is distressing?"

"Job," she corrected, quietly hoping to stop his liquid voice. Her head and chest ached viciously, and all she wanted was bed. "I want to go to bed."

Cedun stilled. "Is that not precipitous?" A smiled crept over his face, and it turned her insides to molten lava.

Clarity speared her. Their grasp of the English language was literal. She said she wanted to go to bed and was speaking to him, ergo, he thought sex. Horror filled her.

Cedun was probably the most relaxed and least repressed of all the *Ba'Tua* she'd met. Gia also suspected he'd been involved with Valerie for some time. After all, Valerie was still young at thirty-seven.

Gia groped for his t-shirt, meaning to push him away. The realization of being so close to Cedun's muscular and unclothed chest flooded her as her hands made contact with hard and well-formed naked flesh. He'd removed that covering before her fall into the pool. Heat flared beneath her fingers as her heart rate sped up. "Cedun, I didn't mean…"

He chuckled. "I laugh with you, De' Gia."

She struggled to free herself. "Go laugh with someone else." Gia couldn't get away fast enough. It was embarrassing that she had a serious case of the 'hots' for her mum's young stud lover. It would be worse to actually act on it.

"Rest, De' Gia. I mean you no harm." His gravelly voice set her to tingling. All over. In places where she shouldn't be tingling, she told her errant body.

Now Cedun was lifting her, her wet, dripping body tight against his warm, bronzed chest. If she moved just a fraction, she could brush her aching nipples against him. As he resettled her in his arms, she moaned.

"You are ill. I will heal you."

She glanced up, and for the first time, she caught the heat in his gaze. Before it could disappear she levered up, giving into the need that had been welling for months, and placed her lips against his.

edun had to repress the groan that rose in his mouth as he pulled away. De' Gia was everything he'd hoped for. Her lush body nestled in his embrace and he was hard already. He might be a *'Ti'* but his years of space travel had relieved him of his inhibitions many cycles ago.

But De' Gia was different. He'd suspected that she thought he'd been intimate with De' Valerie. For the first few months, it had suited him to give her that impression. But over time, it had become a barrier.

Then she'd met Da' Garret.

Cedun had nearly entered seclusion then. Only De' Valerie telling him that she suspected it was a shallow relationship and she believed Da' Garret was seeing other women, had helped him to keep waiting for De' Gia to see him. So many times Cedun had wanted to tell her the truths she'd stubbornly resisted. Now she was here, in his arms, and he clenched them around her as he strode toward the doorway.

"Cedun? I don't feel so well."

He looked down and noted the slightly green tinge to her skin. The way she shook wasn't indicative of desire anymore, but something more, and he cursed himself and every moon. The erection in his pants was more than an irritation. She would need healing.

"Then I shall make that pass."

She laughed, but the quivery sound died away with a groan as she clapped a hand over her mouth. The look in her eyes froze his center, and she squirmed. He loosed his grip and she slid to the floor before fleeing from him and into the house.

He followed her into the kitchen, but she'd headed up the hall, possibly to the bathroom he thought, once he heard the sounds of her distress.

"What should I do?" His query went unanswered. He looked around the room, frowning at the sparse emptiness before spying the bottle on the table, empty. He grinned. "Ahh, so you imbibed too freely, De' Gia." Humans had little stomach for alcohol and the after-effects were rather uncomfortable to his mind.

A creak behind him had Cedun turning. There she was, pale and glassy-eyed, her black hair a wet tangle against her sodden pale blue shirt.

"I'm sorry, Cedun. I probably gave you the wrong impression." Tears dripped down her face, and the warmth that bloomed in his chest threatened to overwhelm him.

He took a step in her direction, stilling only when she raised a shaking hand.

"Cedun, I shouldn't have kissed you. I deeply regret…"

"Da' Gia…"

"No. It shouldn't have happened, and I'd prefer that you left now." There was a fragile dignity to her words. One he couldn't ignore, but it angered him. One day he would make her see, though knowing she was unwell now reinforced for him that it wouldn't be today.

"At least let me heal you."

Gia shook her head, drips splashing, and shaking fingers flew to her lips. "No. Trust me, it's better that you just go. I'll be fine."

A forceful and unnamed emotion raced through him like quicksilver. "I will heal you first, De' Gia. I will not let anyone say I neglected my responsibilities."

When Gia laughed it was cold and brittle. The sound stopped him in his tracks. "I'm not your responsibility, Cedun. Go. Now." Her green eyes were cold and distant, her body tightly coiled as if ready to spring away should he come closer.

Indecision warred. He needed to heal her and give her relief from whatever ailed her, yet his brain told him this wasn't the time to push her to accept his ministration.

"I will leave you for now. But this discussion is not ended."

He slammed out the door, grabbing his shirt from the concrete beside the pool, but he chanced a last look through the window. De' Gia remained where he'd left her, but her hands covered her face.

With a growl, he strode away from the view.

CHAPTER 2

Gia woke to the ringing of bells. Groping for the alarm clock with a hangover wasn't a pleasant thing...especially when it wasn't the alarm clock causing the ringing sound. As her brain settled, she realized it was the front door.

Heaving herself off the bed resulted in vertigo. "Yeah, keep your knickers on! I'm coming."

The imperious sound continued as she shuffled in the direction of the front door, and after wrenching it open, she wished she'd just burrowed under the covers. Garret stood in front of her, a woebegone look on his face. She snidely wondered how long he'd been practicing it.

"What the hell do you want? I said all I needed to yesterday."

She started to push the door shut but he leaned against it. She couldn't close it and nearly retched when he leaned in close. "Don't be like that, baby doll. It was only slap and tickle." The thin edge of his voice cut through her aching brain like a rusty knife. His odd accent, as always, scraped her mind in an irritating fashion.

"Go away, Garret. I'm done with you."

"Now, now. You mustn't be like that. We got along nicely before you found out about Floss."

Her stomach churned, and just as she was sure she was going to throw up, a large meaty hand settled on Garret's shoulder. "She said leave. So you will now go."

"Get lost, alien! My discussion doesn't include you." Garret whirled and gave a snarl.

Gia flung the door wide as Garret swung his fist at Cedun's face.

"Go home. This is not an argument you wish to have." Cedun sounded almost amused as he dodged the punch before Gia's amazed gaze.

"Dammit, Garret. Get lost. I don't want you, and I certainly don't want to hear about Floss and your sexual exploits."

Garret flung another wild jab at Cedun.

"Why? Because you've been having sex with him? I know you salivate over him whenever he's around."

She gaped at Garret's words. "I never…"

"This evens our score, baby doll. You wanted him, and I bet you've had the alien more than once. I am merely reciprocating." This time his punch landed on Cedun's chest with a *thwack*.

"You will apologize to De' Gia for that insult." Cedun spoke in a low tone, but it was menacing, and for the first time Garret stopped and looked at Cedun.

The color bled from Garret's face, but it remained stony and defiant. "I won't." Cedun pushed closer. "Apologize now. Either that or I will be forced—"

Garret stepped back, whirling in Gia's direction. "I shouldn't have spoken out of turn."

He moved away and a look of glee entered his eyes as he slid into his car sitting on the roadside. "But then, you shouldn't fuck your mother's lover!" With that final parting shot and a hearty laugh, he revved the engine and pulled away.

Cedun tensed and looked as if he'd run after Garret but Gia placed her hand on his shoulder, not really gripping, just letting it rest there. "Leave it, Cedun. He isn't worth it." Tiredness seeped into every muscle in her body and she sagged.

Cedun moved toward her. "You are still unwell, De' Gia. Let me help you inside." His touch was gentle, but Gia was mortified by Garret's parting shot. *Am I really that easy to read?*

After letting him settle her in a chair she watched as he moved into the kitchen, filled the kettle, and set it on the burner. "You're very good in the kitchen."

"De' Valerie taught me." He stood on the other side of the breakfast bar, watching her, and she blushed.

"About what Garret said... I know that yesterday I told you to forget what happened, but I need to clear the air. I mean—" Gia broke off her words, feeling foolish.

"I have never been with De' Valerie. I have never been interested in her like that. Not that way. Never." His gaze bored into her as if scanning to find a weakness. She could almost see his mind ticking, thinking of ways to make her believe his words.

"Look, Cedun, you don't have to explain. I mean, you and my mother are entitled to—" He was around the counter and pulling her hard against his chest before she could finish her sentence. "I have never wanted Da' Valerie the way I need you. Do you not see?" His eyes glowed and she waited, mesmerized, as he dipped down in her direction.

This time the kiss was far from gentle. It wasn't fueled by anger, yet her senses swam. His lips were firm and sure while his tongue thrust within her mouth, tangling with hers. His scent filled her mind, turning her brain to the consistency of mush.

Her body betrayed her as languorous warmth invaded her system. She melted against his body, both boneless and yet instantly alive.

When he tugged away this time, she mewled with the loss. "Why did you..." Reality intruded once more, and she stepped out of his embrace. Horror rose. Did he plan to use her? Was that what her mother was about? "How could you? You're just like Garret." Her eyes stung with tears, and her heart thudded in a painful rhythm. "After my mother..." She whirled away sightlessly.

"Gia! I have not been with your mother. De' Valerie and I are friends. No more. She is... She wants another." His voice was heavy with entreaty, and she stilled.

Can that be true? How Gia wanted to believe it, but her eyes had seen other signs that this wasn't so. The way he carried bags for Valerie, helped with the house, was always at the factory...

"*Deandara Gia—Sert bana opta quiot.*" His voice was thick with emotion and she turned. Her mind was unable to figure out what he wanted, so she ignored it as her brain clamored to know the truth.

"I... Is it true?" She reached out a hand just as a loud crash sounded from the front of the house.

For long pregnant seconds they stared at each other before they turned and ran.

At the front of the house lay shards of glass, the remains of the window gathered around a brick.

"Oh my God! Who would do such a thing?"

Turning in Gia's direction, Cedun noted how white her face was. "You go rest. I will attend to this." Silent tears tracked down her cheeks, and the fury within him grew to incandescence. He had a clue as to the perpetrator but couldn't prove anything. At least not yet.

"I... I should help." But Gia looked lost and somehow diminished before him. He raged in his mind. When he found out who had done this...

"Go rest. *Go.*" He shooed her away before hunting for cleaning implements.

Right now I would give anything for my Vakspar. The cleaning implement would have cleared away the shards in seconds, but the *Vakspar* wasn't yet permitted for use in human dwellings. So instead he found the broom closet.

Cedun sent a quick transmission to his clan brother Joruzan, hoping he would share it with De' Valerie. She would want to know about Garret and the smashed window.

With care, Cedun swept the sharp glass shards into the dustpan and disposed of them in the bin. By the time he joined Gia in the kitchen she was sipping a tea and an icy glass of *fortiran* was steeping, the green-blue liquid undulating in the morning light.

She put her drink down and took a deep breath. "I've rung the glaziers. They'll be here in a few hours. Cedun, about before…"

Her color ran high, her eyes filled with embarrassment. It made him ache to kiss her again. The need to reach out and touch her nearly overcame him.

"There is no need to apologize, De' Gia. I want you to understand. There has never been an intimate interest between myself and your *matere*."

She ducked her head and swept her jet-black hair away from her face, her green eyes shining with tears. "Look, Valerie is great. I'm really pleased, and have no intentions of getting in your way, or hers."

Then she bit her lip, a tiny dot of red appearing against her skin. He wanted to smooth it away, and his fingers curled into a fist as he fought the action. *How can I get her to understand?*

Instead, he let his pent-up breath release in a long sigh. She still clung to her erroneous idea. "De' Valerie and I are friends, but she is involved with my friend Joruzan. In fact—"

"In fact, we're here, Gia." Valerie's voice echoed down the hall along with the crunch of feet on the tiles.

His friend and second, Joruzan, filled the entrance, his arm around the tiny, raven-haired Valerie. She didn't look her forty-two years. Snugged up against Joruzan, she looked more like an older sister, though her eyes were a lighter green and there was a tracery of lines around her mouth and eyes that spoke of a life lived.

"Your transmission concerned De' Valerie, and she had to come check on De' Gia for herself." Joruzan's guttural tones were low and angry. "You are safe, De' Gia? *Turaa* Cedun?" This time, Gia turned questioning eyes in his direction. "*Turaa*? What does that mean?"

Her nose wrinkled delightfully.

He'd refused to use *Turaa*, ruler in waiting, deeming it unnecessary. And far too much of a danger right now. That hope was about to disappear in a puff of smoke though.

"Gia, dear. Didn't he ever explain? Cedun is the leader of the 'Ti' generation. He's the *Turaa* and his father is the *Turan* of the *Ba'Tua* from *Dirustandi*." Valerie smiled in his direction, but instead of the customary warmth his heart seized as the chill of rejection settled in him.

Gia stood up and stepped away. "*Turaa*? *Turan*? Ruler? Of *Dirustandi*? Your home world?" She shook her head, and her voice trailed away on a high pitch. "Then what the hell are you doing here?"

He cringed at the look of shock and anger on her face.

He should have told her, long ago. When they first met. Then there would have been no questions about keeping secrets. But he had wanted to get to know her. *But then, even that had been spectacularly unsuccessful.* As time had passed he'd let her think he and Valerie were lovers so he could remain close to her. Now it was probably too late.

"So what the hell was this all about then? Slumming it?" Gia's lip curled in disdain, and he nearly closed his eyes. But a warrior and *Turaa* had to restrain himself.

"Gia Eloise! I didn't bring you up to be obnoxious. Apologize to Cedun." Valerie's voice cut through the thick and tense atmosphere like a knife.

"I apologize for my thoughtless remark." But she certainly didn't look sorry. There was a mulish expression on her face. Her anger lanced him.

"Perhaps I should leave you." Joruzan started to pull away from Valerie, but she clutched his arm.

"No, Joruzan. You should stay. After all, we have an announcement to make and my daughter should get to know you." Valerie squeezed his arm. "Gia...Joruzan and I are going to get married."

"What? I don't even know..." As Gia stared at the couple before her she blanched, and Cedun desperately wanted to support her. She swayed then gathered herself. "Well... What a surprise. I mean—"

"You thought Cedun and I were lovers. I know." This time Valerie spoke in soft tones. "There was never anything more than friendship and support from him. Since the beginning, as you know, he made it easier for me to begin exporting to the *Ba'Tua* home world, with his connections. He's also a very close friend to Joruzan and me."

"Wow. You and Joruzan. Well, congratulations, Mum. I can honestly say you've surprised me."

"Gia, that isn't all." Valerie stepped forward and the mask of the self-assured woman dropped away. Now she was an unsure woman talking to her grown daughter. "I'm... I'm also pregnant. With Joruzan's child."

"Oh. Wow. That's like..." Gia stumbled to a chair and sat down heavily. "Ohmygosh! I'm going to be... Holy hell, I'm going to be a big sister? At twenty-five?"

"Well, you'll be twenty-six when the child is born." Valerie grinned and Cedun returned it before looking back at the shell-shocked woman beside him.

"But is it safe?" Gia asked.

Cedun could see the fear in her eyes and understood. She likely wasn't sure if this was the first pairing of humans and *Ba'Tua*.

"Perfectly so, Gia. This is not the first pregnancy between our species. Though your mother is the most... I believe the term is mature?"

Gia winced at Cedun's words. "Yeah, something like that, but I mean the birth...." Gia's query made him smile.

"Will be just like any other normal human birth. But should there be any issues, our healers will be on hand. She will be safe. I promise you."

CHAPTER 3

*H*er mother, Joruzan, and even Cedun had finally left and the house was silent. The broken pane of glass had been replaced and night had fallen.

Too many emotions crashed down on Gia for her to be able to get a fix on any one. Cedun was not Valerie's lover and with that came relief. Joruzan was and that confused her. What's more they were pregnant and getting married. Her stomach rocked at that thought. Her mother...pregnant. Now that was the ultimate shock.

"I suppose Valerie's young enough." After all, she'd had Gia at just sixteen. But who ever expected their mother to announce a pregnancy to their twenty-five year old daughter? "Not me, that's for certain."

The announcement of Cedun's single status had left her dizzy and excited. Until the bald announcement that Cedun was the *Turaa* of his planet sank in. The distance between them seemed as immense as before. Maybe even more so, after the revelation of his position.

She wandered up the hall, studying each picture she'd chosen to display since moving into the house six months ago. Valerie had helped her to purchase it, and for a time, Gia had thought she'd be sharing it with Garret and later a family of children. "I was so sure he was the one." Until she caught him with Floss.

She sent a thankful prayer that she'd not yet invited him to live full time with her.

Gia stopped and reached for a picture frame, tracing it with a shaking finger. There she was with Valerie when she was three, and on her mother's face was pride and love. Moving on she saw another from her high school graduation. *Just the two of us.* Gia studied the image behind the glass. "Always was just the two of us, wasn't it? We didn't need anyone else back then."

The day she'd met Cedun was the third image that stopped her. Three smiling faces locked in a memory looked back at her. It was also the day Valerie had received her first order from *Dirustandi*. It was the day Gia had come to the conclusion that Valerie and Cedun were lovers. She'd been so wrong and hadn't really questioned it.

"I was wrong about so many things." Her head ached and she longed to shower and settle in her bed. So she gave in and opened the door to her bedroom, stripping off her clothes as she moved to the bathroom. It might be 2024 but the human brain still welcomed the feel of water on the body, she mused.

She stepped under the spray, the needle fine points beating on her body. In her mind's eye, she conjured up a vision of Cedun with his hard, flat planes nestled up against her.

Her sex quivered as need jumped to life. God, she needed to either go to sleep or come up with some way of wiping him from her memory. Sleep would likely just bring on the highly erotic dreams that plagued her regularly. The arousing ones in Technicolor featuring the two of them.

On that thought, came the realization Garret had known about her dreams. All the times he'd teased her about waking up hot, or talking in her sleep... Gia winced. That was probably why Garret had accused her of having sex with Cedun, and she accepted that part of his anger as her due for being unfaithful in her mind.

God, how she wanted to feel Cedun touch her. Her nipples puckered like tight buds of need and she let her hands rise to cover them.

The feel of the distended peaks enticed her to pluck at them. A moan escaped, and her head moved back against the wall as she undulated. The water slid over her body, each and every nerve singing out for more.

"Oh, Cedun...if only you were here." Arching up, she let her hand trail down over her abdomen until it reached her center.

It felt both right and wrong, and she stilled. Arousal wound deep in her gut, her body tightly strung, but she didn't want her hand. She wanted a man. She hungered for Cedun. But he wasn't there.

She clenched her fingers into a ball. A sound alerted her and she swung around. There was Cedun. "I... I beg your pardon."

He started to back away, his hungry gaze traveling over her body as if he too were caught in the intolerable burn of desire. She didn't question why he was there. He was, and she hungered.

"Cedun?" She stepped forward, reaching out to him.

"I should go." But he didn't move, though his gaze traversed her body, resting on each curve, the heat in his eyes melting her.

It's a dream. It has to be. Otherwise, why would he be here? Another step put him within touching distance. "I want you, Cedun. I need to feel you."

He swallowed and she watched his Adam's apple bob up and down. "You... I should..." Her hand found his and tugged him against her. "Forget everything right now. It's just

you and me. No tomorrows. No regrets." She lifted her mouth to his, and he was there, matching her taste-for-taste and touch-for-touch. Plundering. Hard. Fast. *Hungry.*

Tonight anything is okay. After all, it's a dream.

Gia tore at his clothing, stripping him, and the feel of his naked torso against hers was electric. When his arms encircled her she felt glorious ecstasy stealing through her bones, her mind hazing over as the mist of desire descended.

They stumbled backward into the water, hands groping and caressing, legs entwining until his hands found her backside and hoisted her up. His erection was hard and ready, and she was hot, so damned ready for him.

The sound of the thudding water masked their panting breaths and cries of passion.

Linking her feet behind his back, she urged him closer, into the most intimate embrace.

His cock was tight against her entrance, and she arched a little further, the friction battering her senses. Then he was within her. Filling her so full she could hardly breathe. They moved faster now, their bodies starving and hungry for the orgasm that roared closer each second.

His chest, bare and hard, rubbed her nipples, causing tingles of lightning to shoot through her body. Up and down she moved, flexing muscles, while he groaned and met her move for move.

Heart pounding, the feel of cold tiles at her back, he urged her on and she gave him everything right then and there. When she couldn't fight it any longer she gave into the cataclysmic explosion. Cedun joined her, the feel of his jetting completion leaving her a quivering mass of sensations.

His hold is tight, was her first coherent thought. She unwound her legs and let herself drop down to the tiled floor. She could hardly stay upright as the muscles of her legs wobbled like jelly.

"Wow. That's quite... Geez." *What else can I say?* She'd just used the man of her dreams for mindless sex. And it wasn't a dream.

"Come. Let us leave here. We should talk." He gathered her up like a child, holding her in his arms. Her body felt heavy and replete in a way she'd never experienced before.

"Water off." The auto shutdown responded to her demand and left them in silence except for the sound of their breathing, still rapid with the post-sex high.

He carried her to the bedroom and laid her down on the bed. She almost reminded him of the bath towels but he looked so grave and concerned that she couldn't bring herself to mention them.

"Cedun, is something wrong?" Gia knew she should probably cover up, but he'd seen and touched just about every inch of her body. Modesty now would be misplaced.

"This morning..." His violet eyes were troubled.

Gia reached out. "I was a bitch this morning…"

"Not that." For the first time he grinned, but it didn't dispel the concern in his eyes. "The glass. I think it was Garret."

"Oh, Cedun, why would he do something like that? I mean, I know we didn't exactly part on good terms, but he's not a man to hold on to anger."

"He will hurt you. He is a jealous man, *Deandara*. He will hurt you if he gets close again." His hand rose and cupped her cheek. "I cannot —I will not allow that."

*H*olding her close against him was heaven and hell for him. For so long he'd dreamed, but she'd kept her distance. Now there she was. It felt so right that all his good intentions fled. He lay beside her in the bed, her body almost as close as possible without the joining they'd already experienced.

"How did you get in?" Her cat green eyes shone with interest, and he wanted to close his eyes as recriminations slowly stole away the feeling of well-being that had suffused him.

"De' Valerie was concerned about you. She sent me back. I used a matter transmitter so I could assure myself of your safety." And what had he done? Thrown himself upon her with a shameless lack of restraint.

"Well, I guess you know I'm okay now." She grinned for a moment, her features shining in the near darkness, and his love for her welled deep. But had his precipitous actions jeopardized the long-term relationship he longed to enjoy with her?

"De'… Ah, Gia. Might I call you that?"

She blinked at his careful request. Then she laughed out loud, the echo of mirth reaching his soul. Filling the empty corners with light.

"Given what we've just done, I think that would be fine."

He reached out a hand and pushed a fine, almost-dry curl from her face. It sprang back, winding around his finger. He took it as an omen for the future.

"Now that you understand about De' Valerie, would you consent to..." He was lost for words. He wanted to woo her, but didn't have the words. He could speak his native tongue but she wouldn't know what he was asking. It was one more frustration after cycles of the physical restraint.

"What, Cedun?" Her eyes scanned his face, then understanding flared. "If you're asking about this—" She indicated to their bodies lying naked against each other. "I'm not sure if I'm really ready for another relationship."

He closed his eyes, pain crashing through him, and self-doubt, his constant companion, poked him. *I have failed. She does not want me, only this physical union. It is not enough!*

"It's not you, Cedun. It's me. I think I need time to understand what happened with Garret. I mean, I expected more than just a roll in the sack. I wanted marriage and kids. Like Valerie and Joruzan appear to have. I was so ready, but I missed the signs. Was I self-absorbed? Did I imagine what was there? I'm not sure. But I won't do that again. I'm... I don't like making mistakes, and that one was a massive mistake on my part. I'm not sure I quite trust myself at the moment."

In her eyes he could see the entreaty of an uncertain woman, and though he didn't want to, he examined her words, weighed them carefully. If he pushed her now, he might keep her for a short while. He'd have to let her go. *For now.*

"Then I will not push you, Gia. But I will be ready for you. Just..." As difficult as it was to agree, to say the words, he pushed them out. "I will wait for you to be ready and to trust. Now I must go."

Convulsive hands clutched at him. "Already? You can't... Could you stay a little longer?"

Carefully, he removed her hands. "I must go now. I have a role that I must fulfill. Should you require me, I will come." In the pockets of his human clothes was a tiny communicator. He'd give her that and requisition another for himself. He pulled away and she blushed, her cheekbones taking on a rosy tinge.

"I'm sorry. I shouldn't have put you in a difficult position." She tugged the bed covers that were shoved down the end of the bed over her body.

He sighed. Her body messages were horribly mixed, but he could only be honest with her. "I want to stay, but you are not ready, so I will abide by your wish for space. I have a small communicator I will leave with you."

She nodded and he backtracked to the bathroom, hunting through the wet clothes on the floor before finding the device about the size of a credit card. "I have preset it to my code. You just need to press this button." He showed her the tiny depression before he shoved it into her hand and dressed.

"Cedun? Will you join me for dinner tomorrow night?" Her words were hesitant, but he couldn't repress the grin that rose over his face.

"It would be my pleasure, Gia." Now fully dressed, he leaned forward and dropped a light kiss on her lips. "Until tomorrow."

Then he left.

CHAPTER 4

Gia dropped into a heavy sleep, exhausted but happy to have finally been able to admit to the attraction she felt for Cedun. Privately, she conceded that was a mild term to use to describe her fascination for him, but it was at least a level she was ready to admit to.

What woke her hours later, she couldn't exactly say. But jolting from a deep, heavy sleep to instant alertness left her heart thudding wildly.

"Who's there?"

The sound of ragged breathing caught her ears. To her sensitive hearing it sounded excited, as if someone were preparing for something very special. Horror and fear choked her as she scurried back on the sheets, her hand gripping the small communicator. She pressed the spot Cedun had shown her, hoping he would hear and understand her simple and soundless signal.

A harsh hand caught her close, against a soft chest. The scream that wanted to erupt was broken off by something stuffed in her mouth. Her fingers cramped, pressed again hard on the tiny depression, and she worked at pushing the cloth from her mouth.

"You slut! You push me aside because of Floss, then you roll in the sack with him." *Garret!* The words were thick and slurred, and she knew he'd been drinking.

Cruel hands sank into the soft flesh of her arms. "Did you learn any new tricks then, baby doll?"

He tugged the sheet away, and bile rose in her chest. *No!* The sound was little more than a muffled *'oof'* as she fought against him. It seemed to go on forever as he attempted to hold her still, but his state of inebriation meant his grip was ineffective.

She couldn't quantify the length of time she fought him, but suddenly the sound of a crash echoed through the house and his grip loosed and his fetid breath moved away. "I'll be back." The words were low then the sound was gone.

The light flicked on, nearly blinding her.

"*Deandara!* Gia!" This time it was soft, shaking hands, soothing her, pulling the material from her mouth. "Gia! *Quiot dest vun garr*?" His words broke through the icy block that filled her mind.

Her senses swam as she nestled into the embrace. Cedun was there, and she was safe.

Tears streamed as her chest heaved. "Cedun... Oh God! I thought you were going to be too late."

She clutched at his clothing, needing him near to reassure her.

"Never, my Gia. Never." Soft kisses touched her cheeks. "You are... You are...intact?" His odd syntax stood out, and a hiccupping laugh erupted. "Intact?" Another laugh
followed.

"Unhurt, my *Deandara*? Gia, answer me. He did not... You are not defiled?" There was anguish and pain in his voice, and it sobered her.

"No. He was going to, I think, but you saved me." With the crying jag over, she was sure she must look frightful.

As if he could read her mind, Cedun cupped her chin. "You are beautiful, my Gia. Let us get you out of here though, in case he comes back." With careful touches, Cedun helped her out of the bed, noting the red marks on her body and kissing each tenderly. "Never again will he touch you, *Deandara* Gia."

"What does that mean? *Dee–an–dara*?"

Cedun didn't answer, just ducked his head as bright red crested his cheeks.

"Cedun?" Fascination threaded through her.

"Come, we must hurry and leave here."

This time Gia let it be, realizing he wasn't ready to talk about whatever this word meant.

She hurried to the dresser, took out some clothes, and tugged them over her nude body.

"Grab more." He opened her wardrobe and pulled out an old, ratty duffle bag.

"Why?" She looked at the bag and back at him, noting the harsh planes of his face.

"He will be back. Garret will not find you here." Sparks of anger glinted in his gaze, and she gulped.

"But I can't just ignore—"

Cedun shoved the bag at her chest.

"Cedun, I'm not a helpless female."

"No, you are the one I will care for." His words stilled her, the bag dropping between them with a thud. "I will protect you, Gia. The *Ba'Tua* will protect you."

"What do you mean?" Her breath came in tiny little puffs as her heartbeat became a rapid tattoo in her chest.

"I have told you already, Gia. I will protect you. You are mine." Gia's mind blanked at that. *He cares that much?*

Cedun tugged Gia close to him as they entered his home. "I've never traveled that way." Gia's voice still wobbled a little, and he grinned.

"You will become used to matter transmission in time," he told her. Without speaking a word, she shuddered. "It's a far more efficient use of time."

"Time I have, unlike extra bits of me." Her voice was a little stronger, and he steered her toward the kitchen at the center of his home. She'd never been there before, but now that he'd declared himself it was right that she should see it.

The small but efficient house seemed different and brighter now that she was there. "It's beautiful, Cedun. Did you design it yourself?" Her neck craned as she looked around.

"Yes, I did. With the agreements between our governments I was able to recreate my apartment in *Gai-Tak*. It is appropriate for my needs." He shrugged, unable to find the words to tell her it was little more than functional, unlike his sprawling home in the provinces of *Dirustandi*.

"Tell me more about *Gai-Tak*. What's it like?" Her bag settled on the floor with a thud, and she leaned forward on the wooden table, her face alight with interest.

He turned visions over in his mind. Where could he even start? His grasp of her language was so...lacking. He needed to show her how beautiful it was. Make her want to see it. But his self-confidence leached away. He just didn't have the words.

"I will make drinks first. Then I will find images and show you." He pulled away from her but Gia reached out, capturing his sleeve. Holding him close by.

"Tell me, Cedun. Tell me of your world."

He blinked rapidly, noting the color had finally returned to her face.

"It is loud, large. Busy. Many people work hard, but it is a good city. Clean and friendly. No one is without and everyone smiles at those there. The air is sweet, with no pollution."

Her gaze scanned his face. "It sounds like Shangri-La."

He frowned at the unfamiliar location. "Shangri-La? I do not know of this place."

Gia gave a tiny laugh, and her eyes shone in the lamp glow. "Shangri-La is somewhere that doesn't exist. People are beautiful and friendly. They never go without, and stay young, never aging. It's like... It's like a paradise on Earth. It was a place someone made up in a story or movie..." Her words tapered away, and he found himself moving closer. Her smile faded, leaving her once more sad, the corners of her mouth drooping. Her gaze darted from his face to settle on something over his shoulder, but her eyes seemed distant.

"If that is so, why does it make you sad, *Deandara*?" Humans confused him sometimes. If they wanted paradise, then why not just create it?

"Because it doesn't exist. There is no place that beautiful in the entire world, or probably the universe." Now she looked at him, and he pushed the bag away before squatting down beside her.

"It is true, there is nowhere that stops aging, but beauty is everywhere. On every planet. All you have to do is create it."

She laughed, and he rocked back on his heels.

"You find this idea amusing?" he asked.

"Oh boy, it's so simple for you. Just make it, you say. The world doesn't work like that. At least, not here." She shuddered and yawned. "Look, maybe you could just show me to a bedroom. I should sleep. I'm feeling a bit punchy with everything that's happened."

Cedun helped her up, then scooped her bag into his arms. "Come this way."

He led her down the short hall and showed her to his chamber. The one he wanted desperately to share with her. But she wasn't ready, so he would give it up for her. Thoughts of her entwined under his covers, with him, left his heart thudding. His veins hummed with arousal, but he damned himself. She'd very nearly been abused and this was how he cared for her. Awareness flared in her eyes, and they opened wide as she searched his face. He gave a small push before commanding the doors to shut.

For an instant he needed the support of the wall, gratefully accepting the coolness of the surface, letting it cool his super-heated body. Then he jerked away with a sigh. It wouldn't be right to stay there and listen.

Instead, he planned how to capture the man who would have forced his gentle Gia. His hand curved around the communicator in his pocket. If it hadn't been for that... His mind blanked. "Never again." He depressed the button. "Joruzan, we must talk."

*G*ia woke, the sound of singing birds and the warmth of the sun's rays impinging on her. Careful stretches reminded her of aches, not the pleasant I've-been-satisfied variety though, and for a moment her brain stopped functioning. Her eyes settled on the unfamiliar room and the covers reminded her of... Cedun!

"Oh God!" Sitting bolt upright, she ran her fingers down her chest, feeling the rasp of the t-shirt she'd hastily drawn from her dresser the night before.

Horror rose, oily black waves that threatened to consume her before her memories resurfaced. Cedun had saved her. He'd arrived before Garret could—her mind shied away from the ugly word.

She rose, her feet sinking into the pile of the carpet, thick and rich, and she padded to the doorway which opened automatically. The door retracted silently, and she glanced down the hallway.

A computer-generated voice surprised her. "Cedun sends his greetings and requests your company in the kitchen."

"He sends his greetings, huh?" She giggled, feeling like she was in some kind of bad b-grade movie.

"Affirmative."

She laughed, a deep belly-rolling sound, and she jumped as Cedun stepped into the hall. "You are awake. Come, breakfast will be ready momentarily." He beckoned, one hand outstretched, and she sobered. Was she really ready for this level of connection? *The sharing of a meal and kitchen and the morning after?*

Reality intruded, after all, hadn't they shared their bodies—what deeper intimacy could there be? If they'd followed through, she wouldn't have been alone last night and today she would have woken in his arms. All would have been well.

She shrugged the thoughts away as not just negative, but also destructive. "Sure." She took his hand and let him lead her to the cozy room in the center of his house. "You have a computer in the hallway to greet you?"

"It is standard in all houses in *Gai-Tak*. I found not having it confusing."

She laughed at his words and shook her head. So much was different between them, yet so much was the same.

"Sit. I will cook you something filling." He turned away, and for a moment she was sure there was something there, some knowledge that would concern her. But she shrugged it off as a figment of her overactive imagination.

"You don't have to cook for me. Coffee would be perfect."

This time he did look at her, a grin on his handsome face. "You need to nourish your mind and your body. I am sure De' Valerie has told you that many times."

"No! Don't remind me. She always stressed over breakfast." Gia raked her hands through her unruly mop, and the band of her watch snagged in her hair. "Ow!"

"Let me." Cedun carefully disentangled the knot and Gia got a look at the time. "Oh no! I was supposed to be at work…" Then the memory of *why* she hadn't been there yesterday filtered through her brain.

"Gia? Is everything fine?" Cedun sat down opposite her, and Gia rubbed at her itchy eyes.

"Not really. You see, my job is gone—ah, it was dissolved. Jeffrey announced the day before yesterday that they were closing the business immediately. That was before I decided heading to Garret's was the best option. But when I got there and found him in bed with Floss… Well, I kind of lost it. So I went home, found a bottle of wine…"

"Your mother did inform me and so did you. I take it you were planning on drinking your way to the bottom?" His dry tone made her smile.

"Where did you learn a phrase like that?" She gave a self-deprecating laugh. "Well, something along those lines. Then there you were... Hey, what *were* you doing there anyway?" Gia sat upright and pinned him with a sharp stare.

Cedun blushed and glanced away for a moment, but when he looked back there was a glint in his eyes. "De' Valerie was concerned that your pool attendant was vacating...is that the correct word?"

With a little smile, Gia shook her head.

"As De' Valerie is unable to undertake the maintenance on your pool, she asked Joruzan and myself to clean it. It was my turn yesterday, but I usually swim after it is completed, which is how you found me." His blush deepened.

"Ahh! Well, I'm more than thankful that you were. I mean..." Now it was Gia's turn to burn.

"It was my pleasure." His gaze turned wolfish, and she gasped silently as the instantaneous burn of heat assailed her from the inside.

"Oh dear..." The words tapered away as Cedun leaned close, the warmth of his breath caressing her skin.

Below the t-shirt her nipples puckered, and the dull throb between her legs surged to life. Inches from her lips, Cedun stopped. Gia whimpered. "I promised you time. I will give you that." But his words were shaky, as if he too were overcome with the hunger that gnawed deep in her belly.

"I was wrong." The words were a whisper, but he pulled back with a tiny smile. "Never. You are perfect in every way. But, Gia..." His hand cupped her cheek, and she

nuzzled against the warmth of his palm, her nerve endings zinging in reaction to his proximity. The feeling left her momentarily breathless. She was unable to help her body's response to him. "I will give you time."

Cedun pulled away and she sighed. "I've changed my mind, Cedun."

His smile was cool, but his eyes blazed. "No, you just feel the hunger. We will wait. Soon the time will be right." On that note, he pulled away and headed for the cooking block. "Food, we need food."

CHAPTER 5

Cedun used the day to contact the *Tura Guard*. While he couldn't give Gia and her house an official protection, he could and did call in favors. Ones she wouldn't know of if he had his way.

Joruzan also called on connections, including those within the local Earth police. Cedun was pleased he had made such strides with the local forces, but it wasn't enough.

"Joruzan, it is not enough." He looked through the window overlooking the private beach where Gia was walking with her mother.

"It will be enough, the locals have assured me they will be investigating his entry and the attack on Gia." His friend looked out the window. "She seems to be coping well, given the circumstances."

But in his heart Cedun knew she'd pushed the memories away. It was clear that she hoped ignoring the scars of her experience would make them somehow disappear. He'd learned life didn't work that way.

"Have you told—"

"No, Cedun, I have not. She has enough on her hands right now, coping with the gestation. There are also enough who think that any kind of relationship between our two species is...wrong. I try to shield her, but..." Joruzan's words tapered off.

"It is difficult loving human women. I want to offer Gia everything, but she told me that after Garret she does not think she is ready. They lead such open lives, always searching for what is beyond their reach—unlike us. We are taught to wait for our destined ones and to repress our desires." He dragged his hand through his hair and shook away the thought. "As for Garret, I really need to know how he got in her house and how he managed to get away so quickly. Something about the whole situation bothers me. There is something that is not quite right."

"It is like he has a transmitter, yes?"

Cedun stopped, arrested by the thought that Garret might have, somehow, laid his hands on *Ba'Tua* technology. "Could he? Joruzan?" Cedun spun toward his friend, his stomach cramping as he realized that this could be the answer. It chilled him to the core.

"I do not see how. That could only happen if he'd been given a transmission controller or—"

"If he is from another planet. Somewhere like *Galecia*." An icy finger of dread coursed through Cedun.

"I doubt it, Cedun. How could they have even gotten here? Our original thought seems more probable. That Garret has somehow got hold of a matter transmitter."

But that Garret could be a *Galecian*, from the planet that spawned slaves and acquired other planets... If he was... It was too dangerous to entertain without more details. Instead Cedun considered Joruzan's words. "Find out, Joruzan. Check through the records of who has lost one and where. I know we have lost a few *Ba'Tuas* here so we need to find out who they were and the circumstances of their deaths. If he is using a stolen unit, not even our transport vessels are safe."

"I need to let Valerie know." Joruzan hurried away, and Cedun looked out the window, watching his friend striding firmly through the white sand. At home, the sand had a purple tinge, and for a moment he missed it. Fiercely.

Would he ever be able to take Gia home? He knew Joruzan was planning on sharing his home on *Dirustandi* with De' Valerie once the child was safely delivered. How would Gia react when her mother left with Joruzan?

Cedun would have to return home soon, but he couldn't leave without Gia. The pain of knowing something would have to change arced through him. The best he could do was ignore it for now, focus on what could be changed and hope that Gia would come to love him —or at least welcome his request to come to *Dirustandi*.

He turned away from the window as emotions roiled within him. He needed to concentrate, to plan. He would not let his emotions cloud his judgment. He was there for a reason—not to let his needs run riot.

Joruzan entered the kitchen. "Valerie says..." His words trailed away. "You love her daughter, do you not?"

The words skittered over his brain, chilled fingers of ice snaked down his back, and he closed his eyes. He knew this day would come. He just hadn't expected it yet. "Yes. Is it obvious?"

"Not really, not unless someone knows you and your ways. But I have known you since childhood. You have not told her, have you?"

Cedun shook his head. "No. I wanted to. She is not ready after Garret. Then with last night—it just feels wrong to lay this at her feet right now."

"Cedun, you must tell her." Joruzan leaned forward, earnest in his advice.

"Not yet. She must learn to trust herself first, and I must solve this puzzle. Now, we must work."

Turning swiftly, he headed to the doorway, but as he started to step through, Joruzan added a final admonishment. "Love can only be built on truth, Cedun. Many people have lost their chance because of what they kept hidden."

*G*ia railed against Cedun's decision to keep her hidden at his home. They sat in comparative silence in the kitchen on the third night eating the take-away Chinese he'd ordered because her mother had told him it was her favorite. The air between them had gradually become thicker and full of tension. They both skated around the topic of relationships and each other, but the knowledge of what they'd already done was there. Three days of this very subtle kind of torture had her mind reeling with an overload of desire and frustration.

Carefully laying her fork to the side, Gia gazed at him. "I need to go home, Cedun. I'm planning on leaving in the morning."

"No. I promised De' Valerie I would keep you here, safe. If Garret returns..." Silence stretched.

"He won't. I'm sure it was a one-time aberration. He was drunk and angry." She clasped her hands in her lap, hoping to make him think she was a great deal more relaxed and calm than she was.

"It does not mean anything. You are not leaving, Gia." His lips flattened and his eyes glowed a deep violet as he grasped the edge of the table. His body radiated force but she blinked, hoping it would melt away.

She'd known he'd be implacable, but had wanted to do the right thing. Tell him before she left. Now she wondered if he wouldn't hold her tighter to him because he was forewarned. "But I can't stay here. I have things—responsibilities—which can't be ignored."

When he arched an eyebrow and demanded, "Such as?" she shook her head, unable to think of one simple responsibility that tied her. She opened her mouth and closed it again with a snap.

"You will stay here until..." Cedun's face grew dark with anger, the kind someone would aim at themselves, she deduced, when they said too much.

Just what more was there to this whole mess, Gia wondered. "Until what? What are you hiding?"

He didn't answer her though, just stepped away. "You can't treat me like this, Cedun. I'm not a child."

His nostrils flared wide. "No. You are a woman. A human. Someone I feel..."

Gia raised her hand, willing him to stop before he said too much. "No!" Her stomach wobbled as emotions roiled madly inside her body. She didn't want this. Wasn't ready for anything more than some kind of friendship. "Please," she pleaded with him. *Wimp!* The word reverberated in her brain.

She would need to make a decision soon, whether or not she could consider any kind of relationship with him. But after her farcical relationship with Garret her mind second-guessed her every decision.

"Do not 'please', Gia. I must speak—"

She stood, pushing away from the table on wobbly legs. "I can't do this. I need time and space. You need to let me work through—"

He exploded, surging up and moving around to her, his arms encircling like bands of iron. "I cannot let you go. Do not ask me to."

Her heart thudded painfully. "We have a saying—if you love something let it free, if it doesn't come back it wasn't meant to be yours."

The bands tightened. "Please, Gia. Stay with me."

His desperate tone tore at her. A giant lump of solid emotion lodged in her throat. "I have to go." She carefully disentangled herself and pulled away. One quick look at his face nearly sliced her in two. "I have to go." As she repeated the words she turned and left.

CHAPTER 6

Cedun stewed on his anger overnight, and when the next morning came, he rose to an empty house. "Gia?" At the bedroom, he knocked. There was no answer. He pushed the door open. Her bag and clothes gone, cupboard and drawers sat empty, and he dropped to the bed. She'd left, just as she'd told him the night before.

He cursed the sun, he cursed Garret, and most of all, he cursed himself for not pushing harder. For pushing her and speaking of his feelings. It didn't relieve the tension that wound deeply within his gut.

It took time to drive away the tension that cloaked him, but he finally dressed and used the matter transmitter, arriving at his office in the city.

He strode through the small office building he shared with De' Valerie and her company. By the time Cedun stomped into his office, Joruzan had sized him up with a frown. "You told her?"

"She refused to let me speak." He snarled the words, and Joruzan flinched.

"Oh. Valerie said once she has her mind set—"

"You spoke of us to De' Valerie?" Anger bubbled over, seeking any target. Right now it was Joruzan.

"As one speaking to his life-mate." When he didn't stop glowering, Joruzan sighed his frustration. "Cedun, stop for a moment. I understand your anger—"

Cedun needed to control himself, but the acid burn of anger continued to flow. "You understand nothing. By speaking to De' Valerie you have broken my confidence." His hands balled into fists. *How could Joruzan do such a thing? Does our history as brothers-in-arms mean so little?*

Joruzan stood. "I am first and foremost your friend. I am also your second-in-command. The one who is able to offer advice. But you do not need that right now, because you are acting like a child without any kind of restraint. You act as if you are afraid your new toy will be stolen. Stop and consider before you speak again." Joruzan's firm tone broke through the icy wall of hurt and anger.

He was right. His behavior was childish and out of character. He closed his eyes and drew in a deep breath, letting his lungs expand. "Forgive me, Joruzan, for you are right. I have spoken irrationally and acted without restraint."

Joruzan didn't smile, but extended his hand, placing it on Cedun's arm. "Love is tough, and it is harder with the women of Earth. They do not understand how it drives us. They have little knowledge of our culture, so they cannot perceive how deeply we are affected. Now come. We have work to do."

As far as accepting his apology, it really wasn't much, but Cedun accepted Joruzan's words and settled into the small desk area. "Do we have any information on the missing matter transmitters?"

Joruzan returned to his desk and picked up a sheaf of papers. "These are the printouts I requested from our people and the authorities. It is worse than we could have imagined. Forty-three units are missing and cannot be accounted for."

The pit in Cedun's belly grew larger and heavier. "How can there be that many?"

"It is simple. They get misplaced, go missing from pockets in the streets, are filched by women of the night our men frequent."

Cedun started at that. "Women of the…"

"Indeed. It seems several of our number have used them on a regular basis." Joruzan spoke evenly, but Cedun couldn't compute or understand this need some of their number had admitted to.

"I want to know how many there are, Joruzan, and their names. No woman—" Joruzan's raised hand stopped Cedun in his tracks. "Women here can and do participate in this trade openly. They are breaking no rules. It is perfectly legal, and I gather it is quite enjoyable."

Cedun heard the underlying message in Joruzan's voice. *Leave it be.* It went against the teachings and culture of the *Ba'Tua*. Sex was only reserved for mated couples. Indeed, his own responses to Gia broke those rules too, but he planned to mate with her later, when she was ready to accept him, unlike his men who engaged in such trade.

Joruzan pulled out the chair opposite him and sat down heavily. "Others have disappeared in drains. And four of our *Ba'Tua* have passed in suspicious circumstances, accounting for more."

Cedun rubbed his now aching temples. With a contingent of fifteen thousand *Ba'Tua* on this continent alone, he supposed it was to be expected. "We have attempted to triangulate their positions?"

"Yes. I have men tackling that as we speak. I believe some will come to light as the auto-ping generates, but it will not account for all." Joruzan leaned forward. "I've also sent two men to seek Garret and shadow him. If we can get a lock on his location, we may be able to pinpoint which of the transmitters he has managed to get hold of and track him." Joruzan smiled. The grin was cold, and Cedun had a suspicion as to what his friend was planning. The glint in Joruzan's eyes made Cedun smile.

"Then we find him?"

"I believe, *Turaa Cedun*, that would be in order."

"That would certainly answer one question, but another still remains. One that concerns me greatly."

Joruzan inclined his head. "And what would that be?"

"Why does he want Gia so badly that he would attack her in her own home?" For that question, neither had an answer.

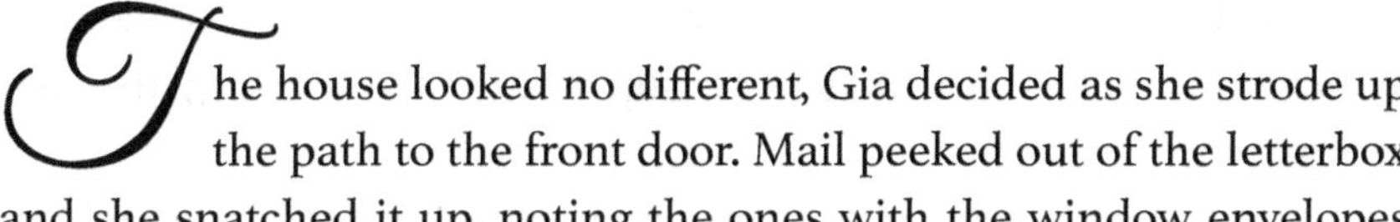

The house looked no different, Gia decided as she strode up the path to the front door. Mail peeked out of the letterbox and she snatched it up, noting the ones with the window envelopes that were clearly bills. "How the hell am I supposed to pay these?"

No job, no future of a job, and bills coming in. Just as well she had no dependents. At least, right now, she had her savings. Had it been like that for Valerie? Had she fretted over each dollar expended? Gia couldn't remember her mother being anything other than loving and giving her full attention to her child, but with the hindsight of adulthood, Gia recognized it must have been a struggle from week to week.

The garden suffered slightly from neglect. Four days without water in high summer left the grass with a brown tinge, and the flowers were decidedly droopy. She'd have to water them later today. Right now, she wanted a coffee and to sit down in the kitchen. To think over what had happened in the last few days and just be by herself.

Cedun had been an excellent host, but she'd been jittery and on edge. Then last night... She blanked that out. "I'm not ready to think about that." The words sounded false as she

said them and she sighed. Was she being ridiculous? What he offered was tantalizing. Sex, a stable relationship... But it sounded too good. "You thought you knew what you were getting into with Garret and look how that turned out."

She firmed her resolve and fished around in her bag, searching for her key, and was slotting it into the lock when a sound caught her attention.

She started to spin around, but a hand clamped over her mouth while another held her hands firmly by her side. "Well now, baby cakes. It's just you and me again. How's about we head inside for a chat?"

She trembled, the sound of his voice so close to her ear and the firm way he held her were effective. Fear flashed, drowning out the voice that screamed in her mind that if he got her inside, who knew what he'd do to her. Gia fumbled with the lock, the sound of panting in her ear causing her fingers to slip and shake. Finally, the key turned.

Once the door was open he shoved her inside, and she stumbled against the cool wall then spun to face him. "What do you want, Garret? You really shouldn't be here." Carefully, trying not to draw his attention, she slid her hand toward her pocket.

"Stay still, baby doll, and let me check your pockets. Don't want you spoiling our party with interlopers, now do we?" There was some kind of amusement in his voice, but it frightened her with the silky dark tones.

Oh God! He's worked it out! He knows I have a communicator.

Garret advanced, but this time she was ready for him and swung her bag up. It carried her clothes, shoes, and purse so the weight should hit with decent force. Somehow she must have telegraphed what she planned to do. He blocked the connection with his hand and the bag jangled angrily, but it gave her time to push against him, out the door. Escape, her mind screamed, and she followed the urge.

Even as she ran, her fingers searched for and found the tiny communicator shoved deep into her pocket. She pressed the notch, desperate to escape Garret, but his hand latched onto her upper arm. An angry jerk with biting fingers had her crying out. Pain arced then her hand numbed as the blood supply to her fingers was compromised. The communicator fell from her hand and he stomped it. It smashed to pieces beneath her horrified gaze, and he looked up, a feral smile flashing over his face.

Gia twisted and dropped her bag, running blindly now. *Garret wants to hurt me. It wasn't just the alcohol.* Fear lashed at her mind as she pounded the asphalt beneath her feet, hoping to flee. There was a shop ahead. Surely someone would help her.

The same bruising grip tugged her close once more. "No escaping this time, you bitch." Screeching filled the air and the blare of a horn. She was released and fell to the ground, crying out as pebbles embedded themselves in her knees and the tender palms of her hands. She

cowered, afraid to look up as a horn blasted once more.

"Hey, lady! Are you okay?"

A vehicle has stopped beside her, the black wheels filling her vision. "I'm... I don't..." Heart thudding, she looked around, realizing that Garret was gone. A light-headed sensation assailed her, and she dipped and swayed even as she reached out for support. The metal of the car was cool but couldn't fight back the gray cloud that appeared around the edges of her sight. Black dots filled her vision and her grip on reality receded a little further.

"Lady? Hey!" The man in the car was opening the door, hurrying out even as she fainted.

Chapter 7

The tiny buzz broke Cedun's concentration and the name flashed before him on the screen before the connection broke off. *Gia!*

He tried to reconnect to the communicator but it failed. Emotions stirred inside him, and he shoved himself out of the chair.

Joruzan raised his startled face. "Something is wrong?"

"I do not know. Gia tried to contact me, then..." His heart thudded in his chest while fear wrapped around him, sinking its claws in deep.

"Location?" Joruzan reached for the tiny stunning weapon they were authorized to carry in their official hours.

Gia wouldn't contact him without a damned good reason. "Where the hell is Garret?" Joruzan opened his mouth, but Cedun shook his head. "I'm heading to Gia's. That is where I think she would have gone. Contact me if you find out anything else." He gripped the transmitter in his hand, hoping like hell he was on the right track.

The world dropped away, and when it came back into view, Cedun was in Gia's doorway, looking at the open door. Her keys and a batch of letters lay scattered on the tiles. Fury bloomed. *Garret. Damn him!*

A commotion in the street caught his eye. There was a knot of people gathered around a car. Something was on the ground and people crowded in.

"Gia!" he bellowed as he set off running. Cedun shouldered his way through the crowd that had formed and found Gia lying on the ground. An icy fear shivered through his brain. *Is she alive?* The need to hear that she was drove him forward.

Her head was cradled in a stranger's lap. "Hey, take it easy, man." Someone in the crowd gripped his shoulder as he surged forward.

"Gia!" His voice was hoarse with fear, and the man cradling her looked at him.

"You know her?" The man pinned him with a cold glare and he nodded, unable to trust his voice.

"She was running like a bat outta hell, and someone was following her, then whoever it was disappeared. Like one of those bloody aliens, you know? Bastards shouldn't be allowed near humans." His voice died away as Cedun stared at him. "You're one of them!" Now there was accusation and fear.

"Is Gia..." He couldn't bring himself to say the words as he brushed away the man's anger.

"She's alive, no thanks to you bastards." The man reached out for Gia as he rose from the ground. "You should go back where you came from! You have no business—"

"Police!" A voice cut through the angry mutters that surrounded them. "Move back! Stand aside."

The crowd parted, and a small man entered the circle.

"You are law enforcement?" Cedun asked.

The man smiled. "Sure am. Someone called us and said a lady had been attacked." He squatted down beside Gia and checked her pulse. "Well, at least she's alive. The ambulance has been called. Anyone here know her name?"

"Gia. Gia Montgomery." The words tumbled from his mouth that felt desiccated. "And you are..." The policeman turned pale blue eyes in his direction and Cedun scowled.

"*Turaa* Cedun of *Dirustandi*."

The man blinked, no doubt taking in his position before he nodded. "Ahh. Right then, *Turaa*, we will need to clear the area so the ambulance can pull in." He scanned the people gathered around. "Folks, thanks for your concern, but we'll take it from here." His voice was forceful enough to make them step back. They murmured and moved away in small groups.

"We do not need the ambulance. I will call my healer and her mother." Cedun spoke carefully, reaching for the communicator.

The policeman sized him up and stopped his movements with a careful hand motion. "Before you do that, tell me why this young woman should be released to you."

"Because she will be safer with us than you right now. I will take her to the compound. She will be cared for there." Cedun reined in his temper. Instead of wasting time talking he could have a healer there, attending to Gia. He almost spoke again, but Joruzan transmitted beside him.

Joruzan's gaze was instantly drawn to Gia, where she remained on the ground, unconscious. "What has—"

"*Garret*. Get a healer here. We will not move her until they are satisfied." Joruzan nodded and moved away.

Within minutes a healer was kneeling beside Gia, murmuring as he applied healing sprays to her. "She will be fine, *Turaa*."

The words eased Cedun's mind, and his grip loosened as the ambulance arrived. Cedun glanced up, noting the policeman was taking the driver's statement.

The paramedics climbed out of the vehicle as the healer stood up. "Where's the patient?" "Oh, there is no need. De' Gia will be well with a rest. The fright, coupled with the bump on her head, is the reason for her faint. She had a concussion, but I have dealt with that too." When the paramedics started to protest, Cedun raised his hand. "My healers have attended to De' Gia. Now I will transmit her to the *Ba'Tua* compound." He turned in the direction of the man clad in blue. "Officer, if you have questions, give our personnel at the gate my name. They will direct you to my home. Joruzan, you will secure De' Gia's house?"

He nodded.

Gia opened her eyes as Cedun lifted her to his chest. "Cedun? What..." He kissed her forehead. "Soon. Now I am taking you home."

CHAPTER 8

The last two days had followed the same pattern. Every moment filled until Gia was too tired to think and had no opportunity to run. Gia vacillated. Valerie had already visited for the day, Joruzan was working in the lounge with Cedun, and the healer was due any minute.

She wanted to go home, but was frightened. But if she stayed, she wanted it to be for the right reasons. And Cedun wasn't going to let her out of his sight.

And the question was, did she really want to stay and if so, then why?

"I shouldn't stay here." The words echoed in the empty room.

Even as she spoke though, her mind insidiously suggested that she didn't have to go home just yet and face the reality of Garret's actions. She could stay there. Cedun would ensure her safety. The voice of reason remonstrated. That would be to use him, wouldn't it?

"I refuse to be a coward and user." She snorted at her own words before the familiar sense of confusion filled her. She didn't really want to leave, but fear of making the same mistake again held her back.

She scrubbed her hands over her face, exhaustion pulling at her.

Wrestling with her feelings left her tired and with more questions than answers. The one thing she couldn't question though was that every time Cedun was near she felt whole and confident. And aroused, but that could simply be lust.

"For heaven's sake, Gia! Get a grip!"

"A grip of what, *Deandara*?" Cedun stood in the doorway, his face a mask of puzzlement. "Tell me what you want, and I will fetch it."

He was so earnest and caring, and her eyes prickled with tears. Garret had never been like this. In fact, thinking about it, she realized Garret hadn't really cared if she had what she wanted or not.

"Cedun, has Valerie left yet?" Suddenly she had to ask her a burning question. He shook his head. "No. Do you need me to find her?"

"Tell me where she is and I'll go see her." In a flash she was on her feet. Cedun opened his mouth to order her to lie back down, the concern so clear in his eyes. The *love*.

"She is on the beach with Joruzan." His gaze roamed over her, and she knew he was checking that she was all right, not overtaxed or anything untoward.

On impulse she rose to her tiptoes and kissed Cedun on the cheek, her lips tingling as they made contact with his lightly-stubbled skin. Her eyes widened in shock. "I'll... I'll be back soon."

She hurried through the house, her heart pounding out a rapid tattoo. At the rear exit she spied Valerie and Joruzan in deep conversation. She didn't really want to intrude, but the answer was suddenly too important to wait any longer.

As if he felt her presence, Joruzan turned and waved at her. She waved back and slowly made her way along the sand, which puffed up with every step.

She stopped beside Valerie who pulled her close. "Are you all right, Gia? You should be resting." Her words were lightly scolding but that paled into insignificance.

"I'm fine, but I need to...umm..." She glanced in Joruzan's direction then back to Valerie.

"Oh, you need to ask me a question, Gia?" Her mother gazed at her for long seconds before she turned to Joruzan. "Joruzan, would you pour me a tea?" Valerie smiled sweetly at the big man, and his confusion was evident in the way he screwed up his face and leaned in closer. For a moment, Gia felt like a voyeur.

"Valerie? You are all right? I offered you one—"

"And I changed my mind, *Deodaru*." Valerie's soft words and the gentle stroke of her hand over her lover's, the intimacy in the touch was too much. Gia glanced away.

When she looked back, Joruzan's eyes blazed with understanding.

"Of course, *Deandara*. A tea will be ready for you in the kitchen." He turned and left the two of them on the beach.

"What does *Deandara* mean, Valerie?"

She looked at Gia, surprise on her glowing face. "Why, it means *love* or *darling*. *Deodaru* is the male version of the word." Valerie smiled broadly. "Does Cedun..."

Her mother's words were like a stomach punch. Love. Darling. "I need to ask you... With Daddy, was it..." The words trailed away. How did she ask her own mother about her relationship with her father? How could this untangle her emotional state?

"Oh, so it's time for those questions. Walk with me, and I'll see if I can give you the answers you need."

The two women made their way down to the water's edge, their toes splashing in the waves as they spoke.

"When I met your father I was only fifteen. Very gullible and very, very young. It was a youthful indiscretion, the type so many girls make. I thought it was love and let him... Well, you know. Then I got pregnant and too late I realized it was an infatuation. Your grandparents were stern and told me I'd made my bed. Your father drifted away. I haven't seen him since your sixth birthday.

"I brought you up by myself. I always tried to do my best, but I was so young. I had no clue. We were happy though, weren't we? We got by. As you got older, I knew this day would come, but no matter how many times I tried to reach your father, he refused my contact." She sighed and looked into the horizon, and for the first time, Gia understood exactly what she'd given up.

"You were only a child yourself."

Valerie smiled at her, raising a hand to her cheek. "But I had a child. One I loved very much. I still do. You are my world, but it's expanding now." She grinned and cupped her hand to the small mound of her belly. "Your brother or sister will need me too."

"I know. But...With Joruzan, how did you know it was...you know, love? Was there like a blinding flash of knowledge or..."

Valerie laughed. "Joruzan sideswiped me. He was there, shadowing me. Doing things for me that I didn't even realize would make my life easier. He was kind but insistent. He just wouldn't take no for an answer." Valerie shook her head. "I couldn't work it out. It made no sense. Here I am a middle-aged woman and he loves me." She shrugged. "Then one day I knew. It just... It just happened." Her voice tapered away and she smiled in an absent fashion, as if remembering things she wasn't able to share.

"But the confusion? The need to not take advantage. Were they there too?" Gia desperately needed guidance.

"It was, but it was more than that. It was just being together, even in the same room, that made everything seem right. It was the little things that counted the most. It was that feeling deep inside that I wanted to be with him."

Gia nodded at her mother's words. She could identify all those things and so much more with Cedun.

"I think I love Cedun."

Valerie took her hands. "Think or know?"

It crystalized in her mind. "Know. I love him. I want to be with him. I want to share everything with him, but I'm afraid. I don't want to hurt him. I don't want him to think it's because of Garret and the care he's taking of me." The words tumbled out, and Valerie slipped Gia's hand in the crook of her elbow.

"When the time is right, the things that need to be said will be spoken." Valerie's eyes searched her face, as if there were more. Gia waited. "If you want one piece of advice?"

Gia nodded. "I could do with any and all advice right now."

"Fine. Gia, you're a good girl, but you take a long time to act.

You've a cautious soul. Cedun is only here for another few months, then he is being recalled. His father wants him to report directly to their senate and take up his position in their society. To do the things a *Turaa* should be doing. So what I'm trying to say is… Don't take too long to act, okay?"

Mulling Valerie's words over, she allowed herself to be turned and they walked back up the beach in the direction of the house.

Cedun placed the file in the tray and prepared to log out of the systems for the night.

Since Gia had returned, his days had dragged. All he thought of was being home. With Gia.

It was intriguing, he mused. Never before had he felt this sense of well-being. He'd been all about the best decisions for his people. Now that warred with his need to be with Gia.

He rose, unable to contain his smile. It was time to go home. Tonight he planned to woo her. Since her chat with Valerie, she'd seemed different. Changed. More open to any kind of connection between them.

Last night he'd kissed her and she'd welcomed his touch. His groin tightened at the memory. *What will tonight bring?*

"Garret is searching for Gia." Joruzan pinned Cedun with a harsh stare, and he controlled the surge of adrenaline. "He is not human, Cedun. He is an AWOL warrior from the *Galecian* Empire."

"What?" Cedun turned around swiftly, needing to check that Joruzan wasn't telling him a joke. But his long years of association reminded him that if Joruzan was saying this, it must be true.

The *Galecian* Empire was an acquisitive race, looking for both habited and uninhabited planets to annex. Earth would be right up their alley—rich with mineral resources and potential slaves.

"Why would he be seeking Gia in particular? This mess makes no sense." Cedun pounded the table.

"No, it does not. But what it does do is explain the transmitter.

They have their own technology, but I have managed to acquire their frequency waves. I might be able to pinpoint him using the tech-signature."

Anger built, a raging hot inferno. "Do it. We need to find Garret before he can get to Gia, and I want to know more about his actions. Why a *Galecian* warrior is here and what their plans are."

"Valerie and Gia?"

Cedun frowned. "We will need to ensure they are secured." Joruzan shoved something into his hand. "What's this?" Cedun asked.

"Personal Placement Locators. I have had some of our tech specialists working on this. They are subdermal, but using one of our matter transmitters, I believe they can be embedded with little or no trauma."

Cedun turned it over in his hands. The tiny transmitters were less than a third of the space of his fingernail. "Excellent. Range?"

"Five thousand kilometers. We also managed to boost the signal so reinforced structures are not an issue."

"Good. I am heading home. Give me the instructions and I will apply Gia's tonight. You will do the same with Valerie?"

Joruzan nodded, his face a tight mask of worry. Cedun knew how he felt, his own fears could choke him if he let them. "I will not risk her. Or the child."

Cedun left the room and transmitted into the kitchen where Gia sat, her laptop on the table. She rose as soon as she saw him, closing the lid of her computer. Her smile was welcoming, and his heart melted. Here was the one woman he wished to spend the rest of his life with. He took a single step in her direction.

A pink blush stole across her cheeks, and her eyes sparkled. "Good evening, Cedun.

Won't you sit down?"

The room was redolent with scents, and she scurried in the direction of the cold box, pulling a bottle from within. "I thought, maybe a glass of wine." She cleared her throat, and he watched her movements.

"Is all well, Gia?"

She gave a short, nervous laugh. "Oh yes. Everything is dandy. I mean..."

"I know this phrase." He stepped up behind her as she shoved the bottle back into the cooler. "Gia..." The words he wanted—needed—to say were stuck in his throat.

He settled his hands on her shoulders, felt the tension in them seep away.

She slowly turned in his embrace. "Cedun, I need to talk to you. I'm so nervous... I'm going to make a hash of this." Her anxiety concerned him.

"Whatever it is, just tell me." For a moment he feared she would say she was leaving. That whatever it was between them could never be, but when she looked at him, there was a heat in her eyes which scorched his soul.

"Gia..." He couldn't contain himself any longer. He needed her. Needed to kiss her. He had to make her his. He dipped his head, his lips glancing hers, before she tugged away with a sigh.

"No. Not yet. I have to say my piece, Cedun. Please." Her eyes glittered, and his heart shattered in his chest. He stepped back, ready to leave her, but she grabbed his hand. "No! Not that."

She breathed deep and he watched as she settled herself, obviously finding her center. Her chest rose and fell, and she tugged him to the table. "Please sit. I have to tell you...

I..." The blush deepened and her fingers curled as if she were fighting herself. "Iloveyou." She rushed the words in a single sound, breathing out as she said them. They stunned him.

Joy. A lightness of being. Completion. The emotions hammered at him, and all he could do was look at her. *She loves me!*

"Okay, I'm a total idiot." Tears sparkled in her eyes as she rose, but his grip on her hand refused to let her retreat.

"You are no idiot. You are the woman I love. *My Deandara.*" A single tear tracked down her face and confusion welled again. "What have I said? *Deandara*? Tell me and I will make it right."

"That's just it, Cedun. Even though I've been foolish and lost in my own self-absorption, you've been there, waiting and making things right. Instead of telling you my feelings, I worried and questioned everything. I'm such an idiot!" She covered her eyes with a shaking hand, and for the first time he smiled.

"You are no idiot. You are a measured and careful woman. I love you for that too."

She gave a wet snort. "Right." She breathed deeply again and dropped her hand. "I really don't deserve you."

Unable to wait any longer, he advanced and pulled her close against him. "Now, let me show you how much I love you." Their lips met and clung as raging hunger swept through him.

CHAPTER 9

His hands roamed over her body and she wanted them. She burned for him. Cedun. Her clothes melted away as tingles spread through every part of her. He kissed her neck, and she shivered as his breath whispered over sensitized skin.

When his hand cupped her breast, she arched, hungry for more of his exquisite torment. Her fingers tangled in his hair, holding him against her, telling him wordlessly of her own need. She dropped them to his shoulder, glorying in the sensation of hard muscle hidden only by cloth.

He shuddered when she found his buttons and began unfastening his shirt. "Bedroom, *Deandara*."

She giggled as they shuffled up the hall, stopping short of the doorway when the need became too much. The kiss was scorching, breath stealing. "More... Don't... Oh God! Don't stop!"

Her shirt fluttered in the fragrant evening breeze, and as it whispered over naked flesh, her nipples furled into tight buds of sensual starvation. When his lips closed over them, her body coiled tight, the molten lava in her belly rising to flash point.

She tore what remained of his clothes away, breathing in hard, rapid pants.

His hands tugged at her coverings until finally they were both naked. The cataclysm was too close. Surely her body would ignite as the flames licked at her? Every move and breath fanning them hotter and brighter.

He shoved her up against the wall, sandwiched with his body, and lifted, the slide of flesh on walls barely even impinging on her senses. Her legs wound around his waist, holding him close. His chest heaved in time with hers, his eyes glittering in the darkness.

"I can't wait. Not now." The growl rumbled through his chest, abrading her distended nipples. The touch of his hard erection scalded her.

Then slowly, with exquisite care he slid within her body. The tender friction filling every part of her until she couldn't tell where she stopped and he began. Tears leaked from between her tightly closed eyes. "Cedun! I love you!"

"*Sert Bana Opta Quiot!*"

He moved, slow undulations that sparked off tongues of fire within her. Gia gasped, her body now stiff as her mind warned that she was close to total meltdown.

Then her orgasm filled her senses, sending her blind.

Her fingers dug tight, seeking to drag him closer, to share the sensations that flashed in her. "Love... Love... You." The words were a mindless chant, and he answered with a ravenous kiss that stole what was left of her soul.

Cedun joined her, holding himself deeply within her as he jetted his seed into her core.

When it was done, he held her still.

"It has never been like that. Never before. Only with you." His eyes shone with such intensity, and now that she'd finally told him of her love, a great weight of concern fell away. After tonight, nothing could ever be the same again. Yet it felt right.

Her heart melted a little further, and she brushed a finger through his hair. "Never for me either. Nothing could mean as much to me as you do." She kissed him, desperate to make him understand,

and when he responded in kind, the searing flash of arousal licked at her again. "I don't think I'm ready..."

Her legs dropped to the floor, floppy and boneless, and he grinned. "To be honest, neither am I. Come, we need a rest."

Her muffled snicker filled the quiet as they made their way to the bedroom, leaving the trail of discarded clothing behind.

Cedun woke slowly, such a feeling of well-being filled him. "Gia?"

His hands moved along the sheet. It was still warm. She was probably in the bathroom.

He folded his arms behind his head, reliving the moment she'd made the declaration.

"*Deandara*?"

She didn't answer, and this time disquiet fluttered in the back of his mind. Why wasn't she answering? It was likely nothing serious, but still, he'd feel better knowing where she was. Especially as they hadn't caught Garret.

Cedun shoved the bed clothes aside, noting the dark green jacket. He frowned. It wasn't his, and Gia had been wearing a pair of jeans and light shirt when he'd arrived home.

"*Gustran!*" Panic assailed him as he chewed out the curse word. He shoved the bathroom door open but it was empty, a towel lying discarded on the floor.

Now he raced down the hallway. She wasn't in the kitchen, and the panic became greasy waves that lurched deep in his gut. He backtracked, finding his pants where they'd stripped in the hallway. His hand found a small container. The subdermal tracker.

Nausea rose, but he beat it back. Now wasn't the time to lose any trace of sense. He searched for and located his communicator. "Joruzan? He is... I think he has Gia." His voice wobbled as did his legs, and he thrust a palm against the wall.

"And Valerie too." Joruzan's voice was cold. Distant. Dangerous.

"We will find them. But, Joruzan? I did not get an opportunity to tag Gia." The truth was, right now she could be anywhere and the thought lanced him, sharp like a scalpel, carving at his heart.

"I got to Valerie. She has her tracker. I was just about to contact you."

Cedun looked down at his pants, pooled on the floor. Without conscious thought he scooped them up and started dressing. "Come to me. We will find Garret, and this time, he will pay."

Joruzan materialized beside him. "I have got the tracker live, it is currently searching." A small device the size of a cellphone sat in Joruzan's palm. Cedun watched as it flashed slowly. The rein on his temper wore thin before the machine beeped.

"Got them! Location of subdermal tracker?" Cedun's heart beat a little faster. "Subdermal tracker is located twenty-seven point four six seven nine degrees south by one hundred and fifty-three point zero two seven eight degrees east. Distance, approximately sixty-nine point six kilometers via road." The robotic tones echoed through the tense silence. So far away.

"Can you pinpoint the exact location?" Cedun leaned closer to the tiny diagnostic device. "Location is accurate to one hundred and fifty meters."

"Joruzan, can we link the location via our transmitters?"

Joruzan nodded and set to work, tweaking the parameters of his personal unit then doing the same with Cedun's. "That should work."

Cedun held up a hand. "Let me grab my stunner from the kitchen, then I am ready." They'd worked together before, so Joruzan was already attuned to the way Cedun worked. He waited the minute it took Cedun to collect his small weapon then rejoined him. "Ready?"

Cedun nodded, and together they depressed the transmission buttons and the world melted away.

CHAPTER 10

The room was small—tiny really. Valerie lay on the bed, her mouth, hands, and feet bound tightly. Her eyes were dagger points of blue fire, and Gia was pleased they weren't aimed at her. Gia wanted to comfort her and get away, but she too was firmly tied to a chair. Only her mouth was free.

"It's okay, Valerie. I'm sure Joruzan and Cedun will come looking for us." Valerie blinked furiously at her and muffled something.

"That's exactly what I was hoping for." The door before her had opened while she'd been trying to settle her mother.

"Why? Why, Garret? I mean, you had me before and Cedun's presence never seemed to bother you. You were the one that took off with Floss."

He leered and her stomach rolled at the foul smell that emanated from his mouth. He laughed into her face, and she shrank away. "It was never really about you, baby cakes. You were just the sexy icing on top. Every time I used your luscious little body I was slamming it home to the *Ba'Tua*. See, Lover Boy was always bad at hiding his emotions. He wanted you and I had you. It was just unfortunate things came to a head earlier than I planned." Garret shrugged, and Gia's mouth dried a little more.

"What do you mean? Did you know Cedun before?" But Cedun had never mentioned him. Another layer of confusion piled up.

"The *Turaa* would never know me. I'm just a lackey. A half *Galecian* lackey at that. Less than the dirt beneath his feet. I grew up on *Dirustandi*, the son of a human whore, who sold herself to a *Ba'Tua* after she stole me from my father. He'd found her in a slave market. All he wanted was that she pay for her way with her body. She ran away with a *Ba'Tuan* freighter crew. But I knew and remembered. My roots were always *Galecian*. When the time came, I made contact and they took me home. Trained me. Gave me purpose. Then they set me free." The far-away look in his eyes wasn't sane, she didn't think. It froze the marrow in her bones.

Garret turned away, and for the first time Gia noted the lank greasy hair and stale sweat that filled the air. This wasn't the Garret she knew, and that made him all the more dangerous. "What... What did they train you for?" It was like picking at a scab, each new piece of information hurt and scared her, but she needed to know. Once she had all the information maybe she could plan a way to get herself and Valerie free.

"You're just a dumb human, happy to live in your secure little bubble. You were happily ignorant of others who want what you have. We need your resources, so I was sent ahead as an advance scout. Then the *Ba'Tua* arrived." He smiled, a cold uptick of thin lips. "That's when I saw him. I saw the way he looked at you and knew it was time for my personal vengeance on the *Ba'Tua* and on him."

Stall him. Play for time. Find something that will give me an edge and maybe he'll change his mind. Gia's eyes flicked back and forth, looking for potential weapons. Hints. Anything that would help end this growing nightmare. "You don't sound like—"

"Like the *Ba'Tua*? Why would I want to? I've been here long enough to learn to speak as you do." His nostrils flared as he turned back, ran a light finger over the v-neck of the thin nightshirt she'd covered herself with when he'd turned up. "I refused to go back, because you are my personal way of shoving it up the *Ba'Tua* and particularly *Turaa* Cedun. You were good in the sack, it's true, but even that wasn't enough reason for me to care."

He whispered the last words against her temple and she knew, deep down, that the cold, brutish nature he was showing now was the real Garret.

"So now you're here. I'm going to give you one last lay, then baby girl, your usefulness is up." The words were cold and impersonal, and she started to shiver and shake. He meant exactly what he'd said.

His hands rose to the buttons of his jeans, and the bitter tang of nausea assailed her again. "Please... Please don't do this, Garret. I haven't done anything."

He laughed, the sound malevolent. It chilled her to the core. "No, but he has. So you will both pay."

Gia's eyes flicked to Valerie, her face so white. "Don't look! Please, don't look." Tears pricked and streamed as she pleaded with her mother. Looking in her mother's eyes, she saw the torment of knowledge on Valerie's face.

Then something was shoved into her mouth and Garret leaned in close. "Don't want you upsetting your mama now. After all, she's next."

Hard hands tore the nightshirt from her body, and she whimpered. *If only Cedun would save me, but he'd have to find us first.* He'd be too late.

*C*edun and Joruzan materialized outside a shabby building with a locked door. More than anger suffused Cedun, giving him an adrenaline rush. His muscles rippled as if with a life of their own. He avoided the fact that Garret had both Valerie and Gia for nearly an hour. That he could have done anything to her. His mind whispered insidious thoughts. *She could be dead.* The thought stole his breath and he wheezed.

"Let it go, Cedun. We will find them."

He couldn't look at Joruzan, sure he'd see a similar fear in the other man's eyes. Cedun fought the sense of vertigo. Defeated it. He glanced again at the door then Joruzan. "Kick it down."

Joruzan, his face set in granite like lines, nodded. They reared back together, lifted their legs, and rammed the wood. It splintered beneath their combined efforts.

A scuffling sound caught his attention and he was off, legs pumping. The door was open and he looked within, his heart thudding hard when he saw Valerie tied to the bed, her mouth gagged. Joruzan shoved past him, throwing himself to his knees.

"Valerie…"

The anguish in Joruzan's voice speared Cedun as he looked for Gia, but there was no sign of her. Fear was more than a cold trickle now, his body felt as if it were encased in ice. "Where is Gia?"

Valerie looked at him, her face pale. "He… He took her through there. He's planning… Dear God! He's mad!" Tears oozed down her cheeks, but he couldn't stay. Gia was still in danger. Needed him.

The door Valerie had indicated was shut, and he laid a shaking hand on it. The whole time his mind circled in a loop of '*Let her be safe.*'

The knob turned without a squeak and he peered inside. There, looming over his precious Gia, was Garret. Naked and fully aroused, ready to rape her.

Cedun's muscles coiled tight as he took in the view before him. Gia was on the bed, spread-eagled, legs and hands tied. She too was naked and pulling at the bindings.

Cedun gave a roar of anger. Fury, such as he'd never felt before, gave him the speed he needed. He charged, only stopping when he'd knocked Garret aside. He didn't feel the impact, but somehow his hands rose, gripping the man at his neck, squeezing.

"I will kill you for this." The words were a feral snarl as the primitive need to protect and avenge his mate rose. *Death is all he deserves.*

"Gggg… Ghhhh…." The gurgle tore from Garret's throat, his vocal chords rippling beneath Cedun's grip. Fingernails tore at him, but he ignored the sting of Garret trying to loosen his hold.

"Cedun, let him go." A hand landed on his shoulder. He wanted to pull away from the touch, but his hand loosened just a little. It was enough for the man to wheeze and his face to lose the bright purple tones.

"Now is not the time to act in anger. Let him go."

He turned to Joruzan, who now stood beside him. "He would have..." He struggled with the emotions that battered his mind and heart.

"But he didn't. We got here in time. Let him face trial."

How could he? *How can you not*, whispered his brain. *Think of Gia.* Cedun stilled, breathed deeply. Right now, he wanted to end Garret. It was like a drug, calling to him with a siren's voice.

A sound echoed through the room. Gia sobbed, and for a second longer the pain squeezed his heart and demanded that the creature they knew as Garret should be put down like a rabid dog.

Slowly, he released Garret and watched as he fell to the floor. The stench of urine invaded his nostrils, and his contempt for the cowering creature grew.

One step back then another, each was difficult. He spun and there was Gia, curled up in a fetal ball, Valerie's arms around her shoulders. The tattered remnants of clothing covered her heaving body. He shook, hoping that he hadn't been too late. That she wouldn't cringe from him. Cedun's heart shriveled at the sounds she made. They were the noises a desperate and helpless woman made.

He advanced and dropped to the floor beside her, and for a moment she cringed then launched herself into his arms. His enfolded her.

"I was not too late?" he asked. She shivered in his arms, and his heart cracked just a little more.

"No. You saved me." Her fingers dug into his shirt.

He let go of the anger and breathed in her scent. "Then let me take you home." He slid careful fingers under her body as the door was shoved open and his own guard arrived.

CHAPTER 11

Gia stepped into the shower. The need to wash away Garret's touch had been a palpable force. Her stomach remained touchy and food carried no interest right now.

He'd been taken away. Joruzan had assured her that Garret would receive psychiatric care before facing the judicial gathering, where he would answer for his crimes. A modicum of sympathy raised its head. Gia supposed somewhere deep within, he knew he'd done the wrong thing. Then she filed that knowledge away. It wouldn't help her now.

Her hands splayed on the shower walls as she welcomed the pelt of hot water. Now she could cry and let go of the fragile barrier she'd somehow forged. Cedun had walked cautious circles around her, and that hurt almost as much as the scrapes and abrasions that decorated her body.

Had she somehow caused Cedun to find her less than what he wanted? Had Garret's touch shattered the connection between her and Cedun?

"It's not fair!" Her wail was lost in the torrent of water as was the sound of the door opening. A gentle touch on her shoulder had her flinching and throwing herself to the side. She slipped and nearly hit the floor but Cedun was there, his arm slung around her waist, stopping her fall.

"You are well? Unhurt?" Such uncertainty threaded through his voice, and it sliced at her.

Gia raised her eyes to his for the first time since he'd found her in the room. "I... Yes.

I'm fine." She felt anything but. The chasm between them scared her silly. Had she lost him? Shaking hands raised her until she stood before him, the water sluicing down both their

bodies. He was still fully clothed while she was naked. Disadvantaged.

Devastated.

Gia gathered what remained of her dignity and stepped back, sliding her arms around herself. "Why are you here?" She searched his face but found no hint of what was going on. His face was an inscrutable mask.

His gaze traveled over her, stopped on her defensive stance, and his shoulders drooped. "I was worried about you." The strangled tones in his voice shook her. "I nearly failed you, Gia. I..."

How could she answer him? "You came looking for absolution?" She bit her lip to suppress the moan of pain.

"No. I..." He stopped and shook his head. "I needed to know... You said he did not hurt you."

"He hurt me, but not physically. Not really. But I need to know why you are here. Why now, Cedun?"

"Because I could not stay away!" He surged forward, winding his arms around her. "He took you. Meant to brutalize you, and I did not... I couldn't find you. I have never felt so scared." Cedun shuddered. "I nearly lost you, and that is... It is not acceptable." His voice thickened on the final word.

Gia realized he'd been holding his own emotions inside, not building a wall around himself. Not pushing her away. Relief and love swelled. "I love you, Cedun. I always will. You saved me. In every way that counts."

His mouth crashed down on hers, every bit of restraint scattered to the winds, and he pulled her closer. When he tugged away they were both heaving. "Come."

A terse word turned off the stream of water and he pulled her from the stall, then folded a fluffy towel around her.

His own wet clothes he discarded and pulled a towel around his waist while she watched him in silence. Then, grasping her hand, they left the bathroom and he led her to the bed. It dipped as she settled herself on the side. *What is he up to?*

With a careful movement he dropped to one knee and she stared at him. "What..." Cedun slipped a finger over her lips. "I believe this is the custom?" He winked, and she

barely breathed. "Gia, I wanted to do this somewhere beautiful, to give you your dreams, but this is right. Because it is about you and me. Our future together. I have spoken with De' Valerie, and she is agreeable." He shook his head. "This is not the words..." He growled his frustration and a smile blossomed on Gia's face. The slow rhythm of her heartbeat sped up. Was he...was he proposing to her?

"It's okay. I think I know what you mean."

"No. I will do this right for you, Gia." He closed his eyes, inhaled, and held it for a second before sighing. Then he opened his lids and pierced her with his violet gaze. "Marry me. Make me the happiest man in our galaxy. Be the woman I spend my life with."

Joy filled her, and she slid from the bed to kneel before him. Her hand shook as she raised it to his cheek and cupped it. "For all my days, Cedun. I can think of no one I'd rather walk beside and share my life with." Then she leaned in and kissed him.

BOOK THREE:
COVERT WEBS

Power, deceit, and passion. Old enemies, new love, and the future of the entire universe hanging in the balance.

Dria is more than the Ba'Tuan Princess, she's also a highly trained warrior who's been sent to Earth to covertly uncover a plot to destroy the accord between the two species.

Military commander Marcus Vane is scarred and weary. His experience with women has left him afraid of commitment...that is until Dria turns up. Not only is she everything a warrior should be—strong, focused, and honorable—she's also an incredibly beautiful woman.

They must work together to find the Incubi and stop their plans, but one split-second decision changes everything, and now the danger is even more extreme.

Content Warning: contains sizzling sex scenes with a gorgeous human male warrior and a beautiful female Ba'Tuan warrior.

CHAPTER 1

*D*ria entered the room, well aware her parents had been planning *something*. Just what it was, she didn't know, but from the look on her commander's face when she'd been sent from the militia grounds, it likely wasn't good.

"Dria. Come in. Your mother and I wish to talk to you." Her father, *Turaa* Cedun, walked the length of the room and gripped her hands. Her mother smiled at her, but Dria couldn't help noticing the tiny wobble at the corners of her mother's lips.

"Father, what could be so important you brought me to the palace in the middle of a training session?"

She tugged off her leather jacket and laid it over the back of a chair as she moved to the end of the table. The knot that had lodged in the center of her belly felt heavy, threatening to drag her to the floor.

A knock sounded on the door behind them and she turned to see her step-grandfather, who was also her father's senior advisor, enter the room. Her eyes narrowed on Joruzan. "What's going on?"

Her father frowned, something he didn't do often, so the impact was a sucker punch to the gut. He held up his hands, and she halted the clenching of her fist, obeying the implicit instruction.

"Dria, we've received a top-level request from the government of Earth for assistance. We've been aware for some time that there is a group, called the Incubi, who are working to destroy the *Ba'Tuan* and Earth coalition. They want to cut all interaction between our two planets."

Her mind whirred. "I can understand that's a concern, but what does it..." A sharp shake of her head and the whipping of her hair around her face betrayed her impatience with the political machinations. *What could they...* Her eyes narrowed.

"Dria, your father and I believe you're best suited to this mission. You're a trained warrior with experience and we can send you in to assist the task force they wish to put together to find and destroy this group." Joruzan spoke slowly, as if every word was carefully weighed.

She turned to face him. "Why me?" The words tore from her. Frustration welled deep.

Didn't anyone understand she had her own plans? Until now, she'd had no need to leave her planet for Earth. Her family and friends resided here. *Dirustandi* was her home, and Earth was some far-flung planet she had no real connection with.

"Because everything we've worked for is in danger, Dria. You're both human and *Ba'Tuan*. You can walk between both worlds. We can pass it off as an official visit." Her mother patted her hand, and while Dria wanted to pull away, she couldn't bring herself to do that. Hurting her mother was inconceivable.

"Why not send Lora or Senra?" The names of her brother and sister rolled off her tongue before she could think.

"Senra is too young, and Lora hasn't the same skills you have. It needs to be you, Dria.

You are ours, and Earth's, best and only hope." Joruzan's words left her with little option.

"But—"

"I know you hate these official duty type things, but it's experience. Besides, you've never been to Earth." Her mother smiled, one of her softly hopeful expressions that tugged at Dria's heart. She would have to accept that she had no choice.

Dria slumped into the chair beside her. "I'm so close to the next level of warrior skills, and Zurah is going to be joining the force soon. I should be there…"

"Right now, you need to fulfill your role as *Turana*. Only you can do that. If we don't protect our agreements, we will be open to other acquisitive species. Both planets need this alliance if we are to stand strong. While we argue, the Incubi are hunting down our people and torturing them. Killing them."

Joruzan's words struck her like a chill. "What do you mean, torturing them? You haven't…"

She grabbed at the images Joruzan handed to her. There before her eyes she saw the signs of beatings and worse. Each photo hammering home the truth. A cold ball formed in her stomach.

"They're doing this to our people?" She glanced at her father. His face was tight, his lips rimmed with white lines.

Her father nodded. "These images were taken three weeks ago—the latest batch of… *victims*. Since then…" He rose and turned to the large window overlooking the township below. "It's getting worse. They're increasing the pressure, and the *Ba'Tuan* women are terrified. The men are angry and the hybrids… They're living in fear of their lives. It's a…" He screwed up his face, as if searching for the right term.

"It's a powder-keg situation, Cedun." Her mother spoke quietly, and he gave a short, sharp nod.

"We need someone we can trust implicitly. Someone with the skills to hunt down these animals, but one who can work with our allies. The human strike team…"

Dria's gaze returned to the images in front of her, brutal and graphic. "Someone who can fight them."

What was being proposed was both a diplomatic mission and a war. She would be protecting the *Ba'Tuans*. It was exactly what she'd trained for.

"Fine. When do I leave?" She rose, her mind already ticking over the list of weaponry she'd require.

"It's not quite that simple." Her father turned from the window and speared her with his glance. "You need to appear...soft. We need to lull them into a false sense of security."

"*What*?" She glared down the length of the table.

"You need to act the Princess Dria. Go all the way. Clothing, attitude, and..."

Dria's stomach clenched, as if she were channeling what her mother was about to say. "Please, don't say it."

Her mother smiled. "Yes, Dria. Hair."

"Oh no!" She backed up, and the tiny smile on her mother's face died away.

Her parents glanced at each other and her mother frowned. "Dria, I need to talk to you. Privately."

Everyone else left the room.

"What's going on?"

"It's time we talked. Things I should have spoken of long ago. Before I met your father..."

Her mother spoke of her association with a man and how it had nearly ended badly. It left Dria more confused than before. "But what does this have to do with me?"

"Probably nothing, but your father and I... We felt you should know. We've gone over everything we've learned, and we believe that before this mission, you should be apprised of my run-in with the *Galecian* I knew as Garret."

Dria sat upright. A *Galecian*? They'd made several incursions over the years against both the *Ba'Tuans* and *Humans*. Their drive to take slaves was one of the reasons the humans and *Ba'Tuan* had come together. Could they somehow be involved? If they were, it could make things infinitely worse.

*M*arcus hefted the pack on his shoulders, puffed a little, then double-timed it toward the barracks. The self-imposed march had been brutal, and every muscle in his body ached, but the gates loomed ahead. He redoubled his efforts and strode onward. Relief coursed as he entered the base.

Even as he reported in, he was shrugging the heavy pack off. "Vane! You're required in the commandant's office." David Mentes, his friend and second to the commandant, inclined his head. "Leave your bags here, and get in there. He's in a mood."

Marcus wordlessly dropped the bag to the floor, stowed his rifle in the cabinet David indicated, and sighed. He adjusted his uniform and strode to the door.

There wasn't time to compose himself as the door swung open and a young ensign, blubbering into a tissue, raced out the door.

"Vane? Get in here!"

Without a word he moved in front of the desk, assumed parade rest, and waited as his superior officer seated himself in the leather chair. "I've received notification that you're required for a top-priority mission. You'll be escorting the *Ba'Tuan* Princess Dria on her tour of Earth."

"*What?*" Of all the things he could possibly have expected, it wasn't this. "You want me to babysit some..."

"Sit down, Marcus, before you fall over." The commandant's brow creased as he gestured to the seat opposite him. It was clear the commandant knew what Marcus had been doing in preparation for his return to full duties.

He groped blindly for the metal surround of the chair and dropped into it. "Sir, I..." "Listen. The Princess Dria is more than she appears. She's been sent here to help us weed out the Incubi operatives. As you know, the *Ba'Tuans* are being targeted and neutralized. We have to find the Incubi and destroy the threat before the alliance is jeopardized."

Marcus shifted closer in his seat. "But sir, how can a princess..."

"She's both a princess and a warrior."

He flinched just a little as a stray memory of another woman, *another warrior*, speared him.

"Her skills are battle ready. We can use both her abilities and her position. As a princess, no one expects her to be more than some simpering miss. Officially, you're to be her guard. Unofficially, you two will be heading up a task force of humans seeking the Incubi."

His mouth gaped slightly as he digested the instructions. "And..."

"Here's her dossier."

A single manila folder slid over the desk in his direction. He gripped it with both hands and slowly opened it. The image at the top of the pile showed a woman with green eyes and pale brown hair. Wide lips and a perfect oval face stared back at him. *Arresting* was the best word he could think of to describe her.

"She's due to arrive tomorrow. I've organized transport for you, several militia officers, and access to whatever munitions you require to undertake the mission."

Marcus exhaled heavily. "Where am I supposed to make contact?" A quick glance at the commandant's expression left Marcus's stomach roiling.

"It's all in there. Read it in the next office, then return the file to Mentes. This mission is NTK." Silence reigned for a moment, then the commandant cleared his throat. "The mission must be successful, Vane." The intent was as clear as the dismissal.

Marcus stood, gave a brief salute, and left the room, folder in hand. Once in the anteroom, he read the information contained in the file. By the time he closed the cover, he was sure he knew more about this Princess—*Turana*—Dria, than his own family.

"Finished?" David hovered, his eyes glinting.

"Yeah." Marcus shoved away from the table, his mind whirling. He had only days to prepare and a lot to do. He impatiently moved toward the door.

"Marcus?"

He stopped and swiveled to see David lingering, his hand on the file. "Good luck." Marcus gave a small nod before pushing through the door and stepping outside.

CHAPTER 2

The shuttle ride had seemed interminable. In the three weeks since they'd left *Dirustandi*, Dria had practiced the primping and princessly attitudes her mother had tried vainly to instill in her over the years. Her fingers were wound into her locks, but instead of the beautiful curls her mother achieved, she ended up with little more than a messy knot of hair.

"*Turana*, let me help you." Verala, the young lady-in-waiting her mother had chosen, sailed forward and slid her fingers deep into her hair before Dria could open her mouth. "You just need to twist it like this."

Pain radiated from her skull, and Dria wrenched herself away before yowling. "That hurts!" For a moment Dria held herself rigid, fists clenched and every muscle coiled tight. As she relaxed she sighed. "I... I'm sorry."

The girl stilled, and Dria could see her shaking her head. "*Turana*, if you wish to make this visit a success, you must let me help you."

"I'm trying. Thank you, Verala. Perhaps it would be best if you left me for a while." The young woman bowed deeply and left the room, the door shushing quietly as Dria gathered the voluminous skirts close and strode to the viewing window. "Why me?"

Of course she already knew the answer. In less than two ship days, they would orbit Earth and she would enter the special shuttle to make the short journey planet-side. She'd journeyed between the *Ba'Tuan* worlds as a warrior, but this time she'd be representing her species. "It's just like any mission. I need to present a front so people will see me as a weak and ineffectual female. I must lull the Incubi into a false sense of security. They mustn't guess the real reason for my visit. I must protect the weak."

The mantra echoed as she sought the equilibrium that would allow her to carry out her mission.

A sharp beep drew her attention. The communication console glowed and she reached out, touching the button. "Yes?"

"*Turana*, we've received an encoded transmission for you. The gentleman is most insistent and is using the Omega code." The captain's face betrayed no concern, but in his eyes, she read a hint of panic.

"Connect me."

His face faded away, replaced by another, harsher visage.

"Forgive me, *Turana* Dria. My name is Commander Marcus Vane, and I am to be your contact on Earth. I've received some intelligence that the Incubi plan to strike when you arrive."

She leaned forward. "I see, and you know this how?"

No matter how hard she tried, the pounding of her blood pulsed faster as interest flared deep in her belly. Her fingers flexed, and she wished for some physical outlet for the strong emotion that filled her. A hiss escaped between her tight lips, and even that angered her. After so many years of training herself to be calm and controlled in all things, how could she allow even that small sign of impatience and anger to escape?

"We intercepted a transmission showing they are aware of the suggested landing sites and times."

Dria frowned at his words. "And so..."

"I have a suggestion that may allow us to circumvent their plans."

Even as she weighed his words, she scanned his face, noting the full lips and cobalt blue eyes. She told her body not to respond to the unfamiliar pull of fascination, but her physical reaction only grew.

"Tell me." She spoke harshly, and watched the way his mouth thinned at her command.

The small bow of his head was the only acknowledgement of subservience.

"Of course, *Turana*. I propose that we bring you planet-side early. Before they have an opportunity to complete their plans. The airfield is under constant surveillance, which leads me to believe they have inside knowledge of our plans."

"I see." Her short answers and demands sounded almost childish, and she winced inwardly.

"You have read the briefing paper?" His voice cut through her thoughts.

"I... Yes." The tactical briefing she'd received left more questions than it answered and anger flared, white-hot. "Contact the captain with your plan, then have him apprise me of the changes." She kept her response brief while her fingers curled with the urge to reach out and trace the planes of his face. *Stupid reaction, Dria. Control yourself!*

"Of course, *Turana*. Do you have any queries?" His voice now was melodious, and a flare of heat warmed her belly.

"No. Send the details. We'll make it work."

"Then I shall leave you..."

"Yes. Good day." The screen darkened, and she rubbed her hands over tired eyes. "*Aargh!*"

Tugging her hands through her long curls didn't help. Instead, yards of material pooled at her elbows, reminding her of the part she was supposed to play. Squeezing her eyes shut didn't help either. Too many relied on her to save them to get lost in her fears.

Dria squared her shoulders and inhaled a shuddering breath. "I will not fail."

arcus jerked away from the communications console. "If she's a warrior, I'll eat my hat." The way she'd spoken...

Closing his eyes against the headache that loomed proved useless in easing his frustrations. In the three days since he'd been apprised of his latest duty, nothing had assuaged his concern.

His stomach knotted as the memory of her face and the cadence of her voice flooded his mind. Interest tugged at him, and he tried to shove it aside. "Haven't you learned already?" His demand to himself echoed through the half-empty room, but the lower region of his body stirred.

He'd been training vigorously with his team since catching this mission, and had just returned to his accommodations. He tugged off his shirt. His nostrils flared as the scent of his sweat rose. Perhaps it was the heat? A shower would help with that.

Even as the thought rose, he acknowledged the truth. He was trying to avoid thinking about *her*. Princess—bloody—Dria.

In the bathroom, he stripped down. "Water on. Regular heat setting."

Marcus stepped into the shower cubicle, and the warm liquid slid over his skin. Bracing his hand on the wall, he closed his eyes and bent his head as he massaged the top of his right thigh. The one that ached interminably—ever since he'd been betrayed.

Memories rose, unbidden, behind his eyelids. Christina, standing framed by the open door, the orange-red of sunset shining on her blonde hair like some ancient Madonna's halo. His ex-lover.

"I tried to warn you. I even went so far as to pack, hoping you would return after this was all done." God, how her final words mocked him. The memory of them searing his brain still, even after all these long months.

When she turned, he knew the truth. It shone in her eyes. *"I never wanted you to get hurt. I just... I needed the information, Marcus. I'm sorry."*

Even as she strode out the door, and he called to her, the rumble began, the earth bucking beneath him. She'd died in the explosion that had damaged his body.

"*Christ!* Women aren't to be trusted." The pain might have lessened, but he'd learned the lesson well.

With a savage twist, he turned. The leg twinged as his abused muscles reminded him of the damage he'd sustained in the blast. A hiss escaped him, and he ordered the water to cease flowing. Leaving the cubicle, he slid the towel around his body and dried himself off.

Padding naked to his room, he surveyed the soulless area. A duffle bag lay on the bed, half-filled with civilian wear. The black pants and matching jacket lay in a heap beside it, waiting for him to don them. These would be his fatigues for the mission. With a long-suffering sigh he scooped up the clothing and began to dress. He had a job to do, and he'd damn well do it to the best of his ability. The self-admonishment didn't make him feel any better.

CHAPTER 3

Marcus gazed over the airfield. The air wavered, hot and close, as the whine grew louder and the thrust from the engines blew dust into the atmosphere as the craft descended.

The crackle of audio feedback blared suddenly in his ear, and he cringed. "Dammit, who's playing with the audio?" His roar was washed away by the sound of the approaching shuttle.

As suddenly as it began, the piercing noise in his ears stopped and the prickle at the back of his neck became a full-blown itch.

It took every ounce of willpower to not glance around. "Check the perimeter again," he growled at his team.

"But sir, we've checked it three times already," the youngest of his team complained. "Do it again, Simpson."

The sigh that sounded through the headpiece told him of the young man's disenchantment. "Yes, sir."

He'd taken the first gopher available, and he was beginning to question that decision. But he'd been stuck. Simon Arends, his distant cousin and first choice, had taken sick.

The draft from the approaching shuttle now resembled a hot wind that seared. He remained still, gaze firmly connected to the shuttle that dropped toward the asphalt-covered ground. When it finally landed a hiss and clank resounded.

Marcus waited for the doors to open, the stairs to be lowered, and the small security detail to disembark.

A pause in time settled as the internal door opened and a woman with light brown hair stepped through. The pale blue gown undulated like a cloud around her as she moved to the top of the stairs slowly. Gracefully.

He frowned. Surely this wasn't the woman he was waiting for?

Then she turned away and a statuesque vision stepped forward. The gown she wore clung to every part of her body, outlining her many assets, while her hair tumbled in a riot of curls over her shoulders. She glanced around.

He tugged his gaze away, but felt the aura of power that emanated from her, and he sucked in a breath and glanced to the side. Her guards had taken up formation, and she proceeded down the stairs.

Marcus grunted with satisfaction before formally acknowledging her.

She looked at him, her eyes narrowed. The skin of his hand itched to make contact, and he swallowed down the unfamiliar throb of attraction. He stepped forward, ready to greet her as protocol demanded. *Sure, tell yourself that if it makes you feel better.*

"Commander Vane?" The huskiness of her voice echoed.

"*Turana* Dria?"

The smile she gifted him with was tight, her lips barely gaining an uptick.

"We should move. The car's ready."

"Isn't there supposed to be some kind of publicity?"

He grimaced. "There was, but I canceled it. No need to give the Incubi a free kick." She inclined her head. "Of course. Let's go."

Stepping aside gave him a whole other perspective. One that included the outline of the globes of her derriere. The blood in his body pulsed hard, as if it were molasses not red liquid in his veins.

Gritting his teeth, he gestured to the vehicle just as the rumble began. The ground rippled, making his body shudder and sway. Without thought, he shoved her, pushing her to the ground before covering her.

It seemed to go on forever, the searing heat of the explosion stealing his wits for a microsecond. He glanced around. The car before them was battered but seemingly intact.

Memories crowded, but he pushed them away. "Get up!" He crawled off the body beneath him, mind whirling. "Numbers three and four form up. I'm evaccing the princess." The other two cars would serve as a buffer as they left the area.

The earpiece squawked as one then another voice acknowledged his demand. His stomach roiled, while chunks of metal still rained down.

Turana Dria pushed up from the ground and carelessly tugged her hair from her eyes. He detected hardness in her gaze and her lips compressed into long, tight lines of white. "Damn them!" The harsh words broke through the crackle of burning metal.

"They'll pay. But not now. My priority is to get you out of here."

"My entourage?"

He grabbed her arm and tugged. "Those still alive will receive whatever care they require. Then my team will discuss with you what happens next."

The air of unleashed violence retreated as she followed his lead. "We'll discuss this later."

"Of course."

She jerked the door open and slid inside.

Marcus slammed it shut behind her and made his way to the front passenger seat. "Get us to the hotel."

"Yes, sir."

****

The room was large and lushly appointed. Not at all what Dria wanted. She'd be happy to be on one of their bases—in the warrior units. Preferably somewhere close to a fully equipped gym and shooting range. Instead, all she could do was pace the hall of the suite and shove furniture out of the way to allow herself room to complete the exercises that cleared her mind.

Vane warned me that they knew and had laid plans.

The muscles in her arms ached as she punished her body, straining as she pushed up off the floor again. Fifty push-ups and thirty crunches weren't nearly enough to allow her to burn off the rage that bubbled in her belly. The shuttle crew had died as had two of the young girls who'd traveled with her. Only the young lady-in-waiting, Verala, and most of the members of her guard had survived. Even so, their injuries were extensive.

Verala had been thrown some distance, landing heavily on the asphalt. She'd sustained severe injuries to her spine and legs. One hip would require surgical replacement. Three of the guards remained incapacitated. Of those, two would be mede-vacced home at the earliest possible opportunity.

The rattle of the door stopped her mid-stretch. She dropped, then crouched, her hand instinctively moving for the small pouch at her waist.

"It's Marcus Vane, *Turana*."

She exhaled and allowed the tension to seep from her body. "Come in, Commander." Dria stood, aware that she wore only a tight black exercise suit that one of the guards had secured from the downstairs clothing store.

His gaze raked over her body, and she shivered. "There's a gym upstairs. If you wish to use it, let me know and I'll ensure that you remain undisturbed." The richness of his voice coated her like silk. She shuddered, and he frowned. "Do you need me to turn down the air conditioning?"

"Uh, no. Sit down, Commander. I'd like to discuss what happened at the airfield this morning."

His lips thinned, but he gave a tiny nod. "Of course." Dria lowered herself to a chair and he followed suit.

"I've received intelligence that the Incubi expected you at ten o'clock. The delay in your landing brought you in at the same time they were planning to attack."

"What's the possibility that the delay from air traffic control was caused by some of their operatives?"

He screwed up his face then sighed heavily. "It's certainly possible. I have some of my people looking into that right now. I had hoped for you to arrive earlier in the day, but because we didn't want to tip them off that we'd received..." A shake of his head told her how much this upset him. "In hindsight, you should have landed before dawn like I wanted, then we would have avoided this."

She understood the frustration and anger that chewed at him. If they'd arrived earlier, then none of their people would be heading home in lead-lined caskets. "Yes, I understand that. I don't have any contacts within your traffic control, so can't assist. Captain Anterrinhem has made available tactical specialists who would like to check the site of the explosion."

"Of course. So far we've ascertained that the projectile was placed at a refueling station on the western border of the landing field. Outside the secure zone."

"*Oh.* Yes, I see the difficulty. They must have figured out that the field was secure." She bit her lip, realizing how stupid her comment sounded as soon as she closed her mouth. Of course Vane would have realized that.

He smiled, a little lopsided, and her heart skipped a beat. "I'd say."

"Well then, I'll get in touch with the captain and have him organize a security team to inspect the site."

"You're not quite what I expected." His face flushed a dull red, and he glanced away. She knew that the words had slipped out, but couldn't control her smile. "I hope that's a compliment?"

"Uh, yeah. Absolutely." He pushed away from the chair with a jerk. "Look, I'm planning on a training session tomorrow morning, after you've had time to..." He waved his hands in the air.

"I'd like that. Say seven o'clock?"

"Good." He headed to the door. "I'm placing men at the door."

"I'll stay here. Not make contact with anyone on anything other than the secured line. I'm going to read through the reports you have made available then try and get some rest."

Once he left and the door clicked shut behind him, she scooped up the thick file on the table. The briefing notes had been joined by the hastily prepared reports from her own people and Marcus Vane.

CHAPTER 4

"Commander, you flatter me." A soft hand fastened on his thigh, resting gently without rubbing or inching upward. The inference in her touch was clear, but unlike most women, she didn't need to be overt in her invitation. His body tightened and he gulped. His mind spun madly as wisps of excitement skittered along nerve endings.

"I'm not... I don't want to get involved with someone I'm working with."

"Commander... Marcus. I'm not looking for involvement. Maybe we could spend some time together? Get to know each other...better."

"It's not right..."

She smiled and leaned in.

Bleep! Bleep! He waved his hand, looking for the alarm button that interrupted this delightful tete-a-tete with the princess. Then he realized it wasn't the bedside alarm he'd programmed for the morning. It was the strident wail of the alarm he'd fastened to the princess's door. His hand slid beneath his pillow even as he sat up in bed.

The princess. The Incubi. "God damn!"

He moved quickly, feet silent as he reached for the door and wrenched it open, pistol in hand. The hallway was empty, but that didn't mean the coast was clear.

He slid along the wall, his eyes scanning back and forth. *Where are my people?* His mouth thinned as he rounded the corner, his gaze settling on the two men at her doorway, slumped to the floor.

A thud and the sound of a thwack resounded and he pounced, punching through the partially open door. "*Turana* Dria?"

Panting, quick and heavy, filled the air and the outline of someone dressed in black loomed in the doorway. He tensed, unsure of what to expect, but before he could speak he heard her sultry voice.

"Commander Vane? The coast is clear."

"What do you mean?"

"They're subdued, Commander." She reached for a light switch and a glow flared. He glanced around and noted two bodies on the floor, hands behind their backs and fastened with some kind of metallic binding.

"Jesus!" The words escaped on a breath. "What happened?"

"I don't know what happened to the guards outside the door, but a noise woke me. I'm a light sleeper after all my years of training, so when I heard something unexpected, I responded. The lights were off, but I was able to get behind the door before they entered my chamber." She grinned. "This was the first thing that came to hand." She held up a lamp, the cord still dangling on the floor. "The first one was simple. A quick blow to the head knocked him out, but before I get around him, the other was there." She shrugged nonchalantly.

Marcus strode closer, noting the sheen of red liquid that snaked along her arm. "You're hurt?"

"Not anything life-threatening. He got a swing with his needle at me before I could avoid him. He scraped me, but I managed to evade whatever was in the syringe."

"Syringe?" He bent and looked at the man. Nothing was in his hand.

"It's still on the floor in the bedroom."

A strange sensation filled him, like the congealing of his innards. "They were after you, *Turana*. This location is no longer secure."

"I would agree, but what do you recommend then?" "We go to the base. It's secure."

The princess cocked her head. "If you think that's best." "I do."

"All right then. You'll want the syringe too?" She cocked her head as if sizing him up. "Yes. I'd like to know what they were going to inject you with. Grab it and whatever you

need for the next few days, then we'll get out of here."

She turned and hurried away from him.

He slid his fingers into his pocket, took out his phone, and made the call to have the prisoners locked away securely. At least until they could be interrogated, then whatever happened to them was in the hands of the courts.

✦

The bed was hard. Narrow. It reminded Dria of home.

She rolled onto her side wondering, not for the first time, why then she couldn't settle into a deep and dreamless sleep.

Two things rattled around in her mind. The first was the situation with the Incubi. They'd obviously decided she was the weak link, and that was exactly what they wanted to achieve. She would use that, and they'd be lulled into a false sense of security.

That brought her to the second and most puzzling problem of all. "*Marcus Vane.*" She whispered his name into the darkness and a frisson of recognition flooded her.

A thrum started between her legs at the thought of him.

"Why? Why him and why now?" She dragged the pillow up and enfolded it in a hard hug against her chest.

Never before had she experienced this flush of interest in a man. Of course she'd enjoyed the odd sexual encounter over the years, but never did her body tingle madly at the *thought* of a man.

Maybe it was her human side. Those who were born of pure *Ba'Tua* families were still repressed to the point of asexuality, but the hybrids born of *Ba'Tuan* and human relations were more open to the advantages of touch and intimacy.

She rolled again, the bed squeaking as she shifted her weight.

She couldn't say what alerted her, but she turned, instantly aware.

It took a second for her eyes to become accustomed to the low light, the gloom punctuated by the light from the computer. Still, it was enough that she could see the doorknob turn soundlessly. Dria rose, mentally preparing herself for battle as she make her way in that direction.

The door opened...

Marcus Vane strode inside, and her breath caught.

"What are you *doing* in here?" She couldn't control the squeak.

He closed the door behind him. "I came to tell you they're using a sedative called midazolam. It's a fast-acting drug that works within minutes." He scrubbed his hand over his face before advancing into the room.

He thrust his hands in his pockets, and she got the impression he was as uncomfortable with their close proximity as she was. She would swear that all the oxygen in the room had evaporated, and her heart beat rapidly in her chest. "Oh. That's not really a pleasant thing, is it?" She bit her lip.

He captured her gaze, his eyes burning, and she had to turn away from him.

Dria glanced down, and for the first time, she realized he wore very little. All that covered him was a short pair of pants and a tank top baring his shoulders and outlining the muscles of his chest.

Oh my God! How impressive are those muscles? Her eyes traveled down, catching sight of the bulge in his pants, but she kept them going and noted the scars on his leg; threads of red and pink, denoting healing scars. Her gaze traveled back to his shoulders.

"Are you..." He cleared his throat and glanced away. "Are you comfortable in here? I know it's not quite the same comfort level as the hotel, but..." His shrug was tight and quick, as if he didn't quite know what to do with himself.

"Yes. It's... It's similar to my home on *Dirustandi*. I live on the base. It reminds me of this." Her stomach jiggled a little, betraying her nerves and interest in the super sexy Marcus Vane. "Why don't you sit down? I have something to discuss with you."

She turned away, sure she'd jump on him if she wasn't occupied.

Reaching for the light, she switched it on. Only when she turned toward him did she realize how revealing her outfit was. A light cami top and panties didn't cover much.

"What did you wish to talk about?" The sound of his gravelly voice raked over her.

She gulped and with great difficulty dragged her gaze away from the sight of his chest. "I found... I found the tracker you placed on me. Or rather, my clothes."

"Ahh." He looked uncomfortable. "It's so I know where you are. For your safety." "Well, it could very well have been the reason they found me. You do realize that, don't you?" The fog of interest dissipated as she aired her concern. "That's why I don't wear one."

"Maybe." He shrugged. "But while you're on Earth, you *will* have one. It's part of our security protocol, and your minders and parents agreed to it." She opened her mouth to argue, but he held up a hand.

"Please, *Turana*. Even if it's just to keep the pen pushers happy." He smiled, and the softening of his face had her close to hyperventilation.

Her nipples pebbled into tight buds of hunger, jutting against the light cotton. It took every ounce of willpower for her to refrain from covering herself.

Dria knew the instant he realized just how aroused she was by him. His eyes turned smoky. His gaze drifted to her chest.

"I... Uh..." Intelligent thought fled as the rapid thumpa-thumpa-thump of her pulse ratcheted up. She reached out, needing the touch of his skin.

"*Turana...*" His deep voice rippled over her, and she was sure stepping forward was the right choice.

The *Ba'Tuan* part of her mind screamed that this action made no sense, as her foot moved, stepping toward the man who intrigued and attracted her. "I... Marcus, if you don't feel..."

"*Ishouldleave.*"

His strangled words stopped her in her tracks, hitting her hard and stealing the breath from her lungs. *He doesn't want me.* Never had she thought that a man turning away would gut her like this. An integral part of her being, maybe it was her soul, cried out in anguish.

Carefully, with great deliberation, she pulled her hand back against her body, hoping the tearing pain didn't show. "Of course. I appreciate you apprising me of the findings."

Without a further word he spun on his heel and left.

A single tear escaped and burned a track down her face. She knew if she called, he'd return to the room, but consoling her wasn't enough. With a growl, Dria strode to the table and snatched up her personal communicator. Any hope of sleep had fled, so instead she'd work.

"It's never failed me before."

For the first time, she realized that in disengaging herself from her peers, she had turned her back on companionship. There was no one she could ask for aid or assistance in matters of the heart.

She turned away from pondering her confused emotions and tugged her tiny handheld comp-screen closer. Dria logged into the security system and began a tactical search.

CHAPTER 5

$\mathcal{M}$arcus lumbered down the hall and settled himself into his room, slumping to the bed with an *oomph*.

I want her. God help me!

She was the only woman since... Marcus refused to allow the other woman into his thoughts. But the *Turana*, she was so far above his pay grade that he might as well be asking for the moon.

She was royalty, and he... He was nothing more than a damaged fighter with a questionable past and not much of a future if he couldn't make this mission work.

The memory of the *Turana* rekindled the erection he'd been sporting since leaving her room. He'd noted the rosebud points of her nipples, the way they jutted against the material, and it had taken every ounce of his resistance to drag himself away.

"She's more than some piece of ass, you fool."

Tugging his hand through his hair, he wondered if the world was conspiring to tease him with beautiful and barely dressed women—first the devious Christina, and now the *Turana* Dria. He'd seen the way her cheeks had pinked and her breathing accelerated. The way her eyes dilated.

Classic symptoms.

He worked on banishing the thoughts that filled his mind by reaching for the file his staff had amassed. He'd start by reading through the statements his people had collected after the explosion at the airfield, then he'd look a little closer at the staff of both the airfield and the refueling station.

The stories they all told were similar. They all seem to have arrived at their usual time, and security inspections found nothing unusual.

Although they had determined the initiation site of the explosion, they knew very little else.

He thumbed through the pages of the refueling station information. He read of the minimal security after hours, that the cameras had a glitch from twenty-three hundred hours through to oh-one hundred, so the feed was grainy.

His people had uploaded the footage and a live link posted direct to his mini-comp. He booted it and the sound of static filled the air. "Dammit."

"System does not recognize that command. Rephrase."

A burst of anger flashed, but he tamped it down. "Enhance video. Remove static." "Command acknowledged." The screen blipped.

What else was there? Correlations between those known at the refueling station and those employed at the airstrip. "Run connections between refueling station personnel and airfield staff." He doubted anything would pop. They were searching for a needle in a haystack.

"Concurrent command?" The voice of the mini-comp demanded an immediate answer. "Yes. Save all findings, then shut down."

The grittiness of his eyes and the drag of exhaustion urged him to rest. Checking the time on the clock, he realized dawn was mere hours away. He'd need some sleep. Who knew what tomorrow would throw at them?

Marcus slid the comp to the bedside table and lay down on his bed.

Without the distractions of the computer, his mind wandered, examining his interactions with the *Turana*. He replayed every word and nuance.

Based on the responses she'd given him while preparing for entry to Earth, he hadn't expected much from her, but now that he'd met her, his grasp of her nature had changed significantly. Dria—the *Turana*, his mind unhelpfully added—was unflappable, quick-witted, and able to look after herself.

She was also breathtakingly beautiful and exhibited none of the inhibitions most pure *Ba'Tua* struggled with. That she had some hidden vulnerability did more than just pique his interest, and that angered and confused him. *I can't afford this kind of distraction. I should have learned that from previous experience with Christina.*

"To hell with this." With a grunt he rolled over and tugged the sheet up. "Think about something else."

In his mind he started to recite the twelve precepts of the *Ba'Tua* and Earth agreement. If that didn't dull his ardor, nothing would.

He only had to recite it three times before sleep claimed him.

⁕

*M*orning came swiftly. The glow from the sun filtered through the curtains as Dria rose. She carefully scraped back her hair, tying it into a loose bun. Then she dressed in a loose gown, tied with a ribbon below her bust.

"Cosmetics next." The daily routine her mother and young Verala had impressed on her during the planning and journey left her grimacing, but she reached for the small packet she'd carried off the ship. With care she applied the creams and powders as they'd schooled her, then she stood back. "Not as good as they'd do, but it'll do."

She slid her feet into the shoes she'd chosen and drew a deep breath. No matter how hard she'd tried during the night to contain the attraction she felt, the thought of seeing Commander Vane filled her with warmth.

Dria opened the door and strode out, projecting what she hoped was a confident air as she prepared for a day of official engagements and tactical maneuvering.

"Princess? Uh, *Turana*?" an unfamiliar male voice called to her.

She spun around, nearly falling, but Marcus, who'd just entered the hallway, reached out, his grip sure and strong as he steadied her. Zings of something close to instantaneous arousal ricocheted through her.

She focused on the young man ahead of her, trying to ignore the recognition of the man at her back. The young officer's uniform carried the regulation pressmarks at the side of his pant legs and shirt. The dark hair a shining cap of black and the blue eyes were piercing in their intensity.

"Yes?" She struggled to keep her spine straight as she answered. Her body almost betraying her, the urge to lean back and accept whatever kind of connection she could get from him nipping at her mind. "Was there something you wanted?"

"Yes. Your vehicle will be here soon, and I wondered what you'd like for breakfast." The anxious tone in the officer's voice carried a touch of obsequiousness. She shrugged it off.

She was here as a VIP to Earth, and it was natural that someone in a lesser position would wish to please her. She'd seen it before with subordinates. There was nothing to gain by ignoring the differences in their positions, except in the long term it would make it harder to request something they were unwilling to do.

Dria subdued the natural urge to overcome the barrier. *I'm not here to make friends. I need to find the weak link and deal with the Incubi.*

"Fruit and tea would be lovely, thank you. Maybe some yogurt, if you have it? I doubt the commander has eaten yet, so you could arrange his meal at the same time." She didn't know what imp of mischief had her speaking for the commander, but it was said and done now. "If you could please deliver it to his dining room as soon as possible." She smiled serenely, softening the dismissal before she turned to face Marcus Vane. "We have things to discuss. I received information from the tactical team."

His eyes flicked over her, and for a minute she was sure he looked a little bewildered at her tone. Then he gave an almost infinitesimal nod. "Of course, *Turana*."

How she hated the way he said that! *And isn't that just stupid? He made it clear last night that he's not interested in you.*

He gestured down the small hallway leading to a dining room. Once there, he pulled out a chair as she hovered. The old-fashioned behavior entranced her, and she had to tamp down the urge to thank him.

She slid carefully into the seat, practicing the genteel action she'd been taught. Her gown slid a little and she sighed, the sound emerging before she could stop it.

"I can only imagine how limiting all that material must be." He softened his words with a tiny grin and she returned it.

"I'd rather be in full combat gear. This feels—" Dria waved her hands in the air. "It feels downright *alien*." She laughed lightly at her words. He joined in, and the cool atmosphere between them warmed slightly.

"So, what have you found out?" He took the seat opposite her.

Dria rubbed her fingertips over the wooden surface of the table. "The tactical team found an unusual signature of chemicals. It seems the explosive is not one that is available on the market here on Earth. That means they have someone with enough know-how to produce their own munitions."

His brows drew together and he leaned back in the seat. "Do they have a chemical breakdown yet?"

Dria cocked her head to one side. "What an interesting question. It's the first one I asked of them. I wanted to know the makeup in case there was something interesting, and there was. They used *cephatic intuvera*."

His head jerked up, his eyes locked on hers, and she knew the information had caught his attention.

"I know." She nodded. "It's a new import from *Dirustandi*. I remember my parents discussing it and the rigmarole the government had to go through to get it on the acceptable imports list."

"So you've..."

A broad smile broke over her face. "I've already requested a list of importing houses and those with purchasing agreements. I've also requested details of the breakdown of the chemical proportions, and I've started to work on the computations for the chemical mass. Once that's complete, we'll know how much was required to produce the explosive device. I believe it will be quite a substantial amount." She bit her lip, wondering what she'd missed.

"And given what you're saying, there will be a footprint." He scratched at the top of his head and several dark hairs stood upright.

She itched to smooth those hairs down, and curled her fingers into a fist. A knock on the door of the dining room was a welcome distraction.

In unison they both called out, "Come in." That amused her.

The young officer who'd questioned her in the hallway entered the room, carrying two trays. "Your breakfast, uh, *Turana*."

Dria struggled to remember his name... Simpson, wasn't it?

A bowl of chopped fruits and a container of pink yogurt fought for space with a large frosted fruit juice sitting beside a steaming cup of tea. The young man bowed deeply as he placed the tray before her. The same was delivered to Marcus, minus the bow, she noted.

Once they were alone again she lifted her spoon and tasted the yogurt, grimacing at the bite.

"Overnight I ran the names of the airfield and refueling station staff through the world-wide citizen census, but it's a time consuming search. With millions of names and associations to check I don't expect an answer before tonight or tomorrow. My people have also checked the video feeds for the two locations. At the refueling station we found a glitch for a period of about three hours. The camera caught black and haze. Nothing else." His eyes roamed her face as he spoke.

"I see. Will you be able to clear the haze?" Her stomach was starting to rebel slightly at the bitter tang, so she shoved the yogurt away.

"Don't like it?" His brow furrowed.

"It's not quite to my taste." She attempted to be diplomatic, the training Joruzan had tried to force on her over the years raised its head.

"Oh. I suppose many things are different here, but you'd be used to that." He spoke quietly.

"Well, the little I've seen is both similar and different, but I haven't left *Dirustandi* for official business before. Or at least, nothing like this, not so far away."

He smiled. "I've never left Earth, so your experience far exceeds mine." In silence, they finished eating as they discussed what they'd found.

CHAPTER 6

*P*acing behind the *Turana* was painful, given his current physical condition, Marcus thought sourly. Watching her hips sway beneath the many layers of her voluminous skirts really didn't help.

She's a trained warrior. See her that way.

He sighed and turned his gaze back to the crowd that had gathered to see her.

She slowly made her way to the door of the television studio, a sea of bodies held behind a thin plastic line.

He'd warned his team that this was the perfect place for an attack, but he didn't necessarily expect anything to happen; there were too many humans who could be injured and they weren't the target of the Incubi.

At the door Dria turned and raised a hand. A smile on her face, her eyes shining as she gave them one final wave. The crowd erupted in a thunder of applause and shouts.

Instinctively, he moved before her, sheltering her body with his own. Marcus tugged the door open and shoved her inside, his body plastered against hers, almost skin-to-skin.

"What are you doing, Vane?" Her husky voice flowed over him like silken caramel, and his erection tightened like a vise in his groin.

"*Saving you*. What the *fuck* were you thinking? That last little action whipped them into a frenzy."

"My mother instructed me that people like that kind of thing. In fact—"

He cut off her answer. "That's just bloody stupid, and all you did was make yourself an even bigger target." He sounded petulant, but the urge to protect her had suddenly descended with a burning anger. "Don't do it again."

She laughed, and it wasn't pleasant, as if she too were struggling with their close confines. The program for the day had taken them to photo shoots, kindergartens, and schools. Watching her 'press the flesh' as she termed it had tested his limits. Being so close, watching her... He growled deep in his throat.

"Oh dear. I didn't mean to upset you, Commander Vane. Next time I'll check before I so much as sneeze." She marched forward, and the director of *Now in News* moved in her direction, a sleazy smile on his lips.

"*Turana*, it's such a pleasure that you could find time to see us. Come this way, and I'll take you directly to makeup."

"Of course. Anything to further *Ba'Tuan* and Earth relations." She smiled coquettishly as he patted her arm.

A bolt of jealousy shot down Vane's spine.

"Up close, you are so much taller and...*beautiful!*"

For the first time, he wished that the language of Earth wasn't one standard variation of English, because the words sounded damned stupid to his mind. Listening to the man in his fifth decade gush over her wasn't helping his temper.

Exhaustion started to cloud his judgement and common sense.

Dria disappeared around the corner, and as Marcus started to round it, a large goon slid in front of him.

"Only guests through there. You can wait—"

He thrust his hand into the pocket of his pants, pulled out a security pass, and waved it in front of the beefy man blocking his path. "I can go wherever the hell I need to. I'm the *Turana's* personal guard. So move."

The man's eyes narrowed for an instant before he moved to the side and shook his head. "Sorry, man. With so many people in here tonight, it's hard to work out who should be back here and who shouldn't."

The news upset Marcus. "Then you'd better take me to her straight away." He exuded menace and the goon backed away, paling visibly

"Sure. They're taking her into the VIP dressing room. It's this way."

The man directed him to a discreetly hidden entrance at the end of a hallway, and as Marcus stepped within, he noted that Dria was obviously at the end of her limits too. Her eyes were closed and she rested against the back of a chair. Lines bracketed her mouth and her shoulders slumped.

"You'd better clear a chair, Vane," she said.

He gazed around the room. Chairs were scattered haphazardly, each piled high with clothing.

"The cosmetician said she'd be back in ten, and from what I understand, this could take a while." The princess slipped two slices of cucumber over her eyes. "She told me this would help with any puffiness. Whoever heard of something so stupid anyway? I'd rather eat them than waste cucumber." She mumbled the words and Marcus laughed.

"Yeah, I've never been able to understand that kind of thinking myself." A large chair sat in the corner, and he moved the mounded clothing out of his way. "I'll just sit over here."

The chair was a conformable recliner, which molded around him, and without any conscious thought he relaxed the tight muscles of his body. Marcus closed his eyes, and a wave of exhaustion swamped him.

"Vane? Are you there?" The whisper rippled through him, electrifying cells within his body. He glanced up, realizing he'd fallen asleep in the chair. Her seat sat empty and a heavy stone took up position in his belly.

"Turana?"

"I'm here. And my name is Dria. Call me Dria, Marcus. I can call you that, can't I?" The husky tones of her voice increased the ache in his groin while loosening the fear that had suffused him.

"Yeah. You can call me...anything you want." He gulped as she gave a sexy laugh and her breasts, naked like the rest of her body, quivered.

"I like that. I like...you. Do you..." She licked her lips in an attitude of insecurity. "Do you like me?"

His eyes widened as she loomed over him.

He glanced at the door. It was locked, and the lights in the room were turned down low. "I do. I more than like you." He pushed out of the seat and rose, meeting her halfway as

their lips collided.

Hers were soft. Tender.

His hands rose, cupping her shoulders, and his thumbs started massaging her. Her skin was silken and firm. Just as he'd expected. The thought exploded in his mind as their bodies moved closer together and his lips worshipped hers.

She tasted of berries. Ripe summer fruits, all warm and sweet.

A tiny mewl rose while Dria gyrated against him. The pressure in his groin responded to the play of her fingers as she tugged at his belt.

He shrugged away. "Not yet. I'm not ready. You're not ready." The invitation he saw in her eyes belied his words though.

"I'm more than ready, Marcus. Feel me. Feel how hungry I am for you." Her hand pulled at his, dragged it down the curves of her belly and to the silken forest of hair that hid her core. "Feel me. Feel how ready I am for you."

Without conscious thought, he slid a finger between the soft, damp cleft of her sex. A broken cry of excitement tore from her lips. The sound stole the breath from his body.

He leaned in and kissed her, hard. Lips to lips, and tongue to tongue they tangled, bodies writhing.

She touched his shoulder, tugged and shook...

"Dammit, Vane! Wake up!" The anxiety in her voice shook him.

"Wha... What?" He glanced around, bleary-eyed.

"You fell asleep." The anxious thread in her voice was replaced with anger. "You must have been having an interesting dream, given you kept muttering 'I want you.'"

"*Shit!*" He realized now he'd been dreaming about her. A highly erotic fantasy of him and her—them! "I didn't mean.... I didn't really sleep well last night and with today, I guess it took more out of me than I thought." His hand automatically reached for his throbbing thigh and he massaged it.

"I... Are you all right? What's wrong with your leg?" Her face screwed up. "I mean, apart from the scars."

He pursed his lips. "I was caught in an explosion nearly twelve months ago. It hurts when I'm not careful." He kept his tone neutral, hoping she'd stop asking.

"Oh. Sorry, I shouldn't have... Look Vane, I just... I couldn't seem to wake you and I was worried."

He peered closer, noting the white of her lips and the way she rubbed at her stomach. "Not feeling well?"

"I haven't felt very well all day. To be honest, I'm glad this is our last official visit. I'm tired, and I'd rather check on my people than be here right now."

"I can arrange that for after, if you wish?" He desperately wanted to relieve the pressure she was clearly feeling.

"I think only Verala is left at the healer's clinic. But I'd like to check on her. She's very young and a long way from home." Her concern, even while dealing with her own discomfort, was touching.

"I'll arrange that then."

She smiled, and it warmed his heart. "Can I..."

She glanced away, and he wondered what it was she felt so unsure of asking.

When she turned back, a crest of red colored her cheeks. "Could I call you Marcus? Since we're going to be stuck together for however long, it would make it a little easier." She bit her lip, making her look young and vulnerable.

"I'd like that, *Turana*."

Her frown marred the sense of wellbeing he experienced. "You really should call me Dria. Most of my friends do."

"Are we friends, Dria? Is that possible?"

She blushed a deep crimson, and he knew exactly why. They were already *more* than friends on a physical level.

"I'd like to think we're well on the way."

"Then, your calling me Marcus suits me."

At that instant the door opened and the makeup artist walked in. "Did I interrupt something?"

The artless guile on the woman's face was all an act, Marcus knew, but he played along.

Whether she'd been listening at the door, or had read the signals from their bodies didn't matter.

They both had a part to play, and play it they would.

"Not at all. I think the *Turana* is ready for you though."

He couldn't be totally sure, but he thought Dria muttered something along the lines of, "I seriously doubt it."

He chuckled and retreated to the comfort of his chair.

CHAPTER 7

*D*ria threw the newspaper to the tabletop with an inelegant snort. "They should outlaw printing this kind of rubbish. 'Princess embroiled in relationship with guard.' My parents would be appalled if they could see this."

They would probably lecture her for days, but she hadn't done anything to bring it about. She wracked her brains trying to work out who would have circulated such a story. The only person she could think of was the makeup artist. And even then, they'd not done anything untoward. At least, not physically.

Marcus dropped to the seat opposite her and grabbed the paper. "It could work to our benefit though."

Dria squinted. "How so?"

"Well, firstly it promotes the idea that you are here totally for pleasure and strengthens the argument that you are merely a titular member of the militia."

"But my parents! They'll think I'm shirking my responsibilities, and my commander—" She bit off her complaints at his raised eyebrow. "What?"

His warm smile scattered her wits. "We know what you've

achieved so far. Verala will return home in several days, and you've ascertained that the chemicals have to be delivered in quantities. This will help us track down those involved. You've already begun the process of investigating buyers. You're ensuring that no one thinks you are more than your mission requires, so I'd say, what you've achieved is quite successful." He shifted into a reclining position and watched her.

He was right, of course. She knew that on an instinctive level, but it didn't make Dria feel any better. "I'm hopeful the information regarding buyers will arrive later today."

"Good. Now eat. If you don't, you'll faint on me and they'll say you're pregnant with a *Ba'Tuan* hybrid."

Her heart almost stopped beating at that thought. That they'd think... "I, um... Of course I wouldn't want anyone to get the wrong thought... That you and I are, you know, involved." *God, I sound like some stilted virgin when I speak like that.*

He smiled, and not for the first time she almost swallowed her tongue. "We could be, you know. Involved." The grin widened as he watched her reaction.

"I... Uh..."

The intensity of his gaze deepened. "I dreamed about you while you were waiting for the makeup artist. It was about you and me. Together. *Intimately*." Red crested his cheeks, telling her he was taking a chance on sharing his dream.

"I... I'm interested. But I have a job..." Her denial sounded weak.

Hunger and lust mingled in his eyes, and they turned smoky. His hand reached out and touched hers where it rested on the table. His touch scorched her.

Without warning, he shoved away from the table, stood up, then shook his head. "What am I thinking? It's stupid, against the rules, and I should know better." He ground out the words between clenched teeth.

The thought of them together entranced her. Involved with Marcus Vane. He'd be a strong lover. She'd seen glimpses of the man he'd attempted to hide since her arrival. Despite this, the fascination wasn't enough to allow her to chance it. She'd been prepared once and he'd turned away. What if... Doubts assailed her.

When he turned back, hunger etched his face. "Last night, I tossed and turned. The only thing that made any sense was that I be open with you. Tell you that I hunger for you."

Unable to control her confusion, she spoke. "Why? Why do you fight it, Marcus? What happened in your past that makes you so shy of committing to a woman? Why change your perspective for me?"

He backed away. "I don't know. It doesn't make sense. After... After Christina, I swore no other woman would make me feel..." He shook his head, clearly unable to share the truth of whatever stopped him making a connection.

The slow thud of her heart took on a more rapid beat. If he would tell her everything, she'd listen, even if it tore her heart in two.

Perhaps if he came to terms with his pain, he'd take a chance on a relationship with her. "Tell me about Christina."

She reached in his direction, but he jerked away, avoiding her touch.

"No. It's..." He sighed heavily and sat down opposite her. "I can't. What's done is done." With those words, he closed down the conversation.

*H*eat wavered, the shimmer in the distance betrayed the temperatures. As he watched, the *Turana*—Dria, as she'd reminded him—moved through the massed crowds that gathered. Bouquets were thrust at her. Lines of people stretched before them, and they called out her name.

Today she would meet with council representatives of the hybrid community. They wished to raise issues that they'd been unable to communicate to the Earth government. Things such as their status in law had ground to a halt several years ago. With the rising number of hybrids, they needed someone to advocate for them.

Dria, as a visiting *Ba'Tuan* dignitary, offered to meet with them.

He was aware that she felt strongly that she needed to find out their issues. She'd told him several times that she wanted to meet with the human government with all the facts.

Marcus watched the way she interacted with those gathered. She had a knack of finding the right attitude, whether it was instinctive or training, he couldn't say. Just that she always seemed to leave people smiling.

Like me.

Was that why he'd brought up Christina? He hadn't planned to. It could be because Dria came across as caring and involved. It seemed strange to him that she was a trained warrior, yet retained a "softness" that allowed her to interact freely with both old and young.

She also took her responsibility as the crown princess of her people seriously. Each person she met was the focus of her attention for the time she was with them.

"Sir, we've received intelligence that someone could be embedded in the crowd. I suggest we retreat and regroup." The voice on the line was scratchy, but instantly Marcus was alert and moving toward Dria.

"What information do you have? I need details." His hand covered the earpiece as he strained to hear. Urgent feelings rose in his chest, smothering him.

"Nothing more specific, sir."

Marcus glanced in Dria's direction, where she nodded at something the woman she was talking to had said. He moved swiftly and placed a hand on her shoulder.

"Just a moment, Commander." A quick grin over her shoulder softened her words, then her full attention returned to the woman before her.

A frisson of frustration rose. "Sorry, Princess. This can't wait." She turned and her eyes narrowed. "There's a problem?"

"Potentially. We need to get out of here." He tugged, hoping to propel her toward the cars, but she pushed away.

"No."

"*Turana*, there's a clear threat to you. If you won't use the car then employ your transporter."

"I don't use them."

CHAPTER 8

"What? What do you mean?" Marcus asked. His lips thinned, and anger shot through her.

"Because in a battle situation, they can be tracked. Any tactical advantage is neutralized.

I don't carry one, because it makes me a target."

The expression on his face conveyed both frustration and confusion. "For heaven's sake.

You have to get out of here." He pushed at her, trying to shove her to the door.

"No. I have a commitment. Let me finish here, then—" She started to turn back, but he stilled her.

"Sorry. No can do. We need to move now."

She understood his situation, but this was too important. Not just to her but also the *Ba'Tuan* hybrids. "I can't. These are important discussions. I won't leave."

Even as he prepared to speak, Dria accepted the tiny card the woman she'd been talking to proffered, and stashed it in the bag she carried over her arm. Dria shaded her eyes against the brilliant shine of the sun then strolled toward the door. She teamed her quick wave with a smile, as if nothing were wrong.

The only reaction she allowed was the bracing of her shoulders as she moved to the middle of the crowd. Her feet tapped as she made her way up the steps, and at the doorway, she stilled, turned, and gave a final wave before she stepped inside the building.

"*Turana*, you're in danger. And you're potentially putting everyone here in danger," Marcus whispered.

Her stomach wobbled at that information. But she'd promised them that she would address their issues, and until she had something concrete to base the decision to cancel on, she couldn't in all good conscience clear the area. "No. I promised my parents and Joruzan I would follow through with this. The needs of the hybrids are too important."

"But the information—"

Her gaze speared him. "You have specific information? A credible threat?" He shook his head.

If she were going to even consider leaving, she needed more than a whisper.

"Can you honestly tell me they're more important than you?" He spoke harshly, but his steady gaze remained on her face. "Come on, Dria. You know as well as I do, you need to get out of here, and them too."

She knew he wanted to shock her into making a decision. Should she evacuate? Without more details, she couldn't.

"Dammit, if someone tries to make a move, you're a sitting duck."

"I know. But I gave a commitment, Marcus. I have to follow this through. I promise not to take any chances, but this is part of why I'm here." Dria stepped back, but reached out to grasp his hand loosely. "As soon as I can, I'll leave. I promise, but unless you have more..."

Time passed slowly as she glanced around from her position at the table. Marcus wasn't a happy man, but nothing she did would make him happy right now. Dria focused her attention on the man in front of her, listening to the issues he raised.

"Princess, we've made appeals, but the government doesn't seem to understand. While we carry citizenship of the countries of our birth, our hybrid status means we can't be registered as citizens of Earth. Ergo, we can't access certain employment, judicial, and political services. We've lived with these issues, but our children... I don't wish to see my daughter restricted as I have been." He gestured to the child who sat quietly beside him. Dria judged her to be about twelve or thirteen. More than old enough on her planet to start learning and participating in formal meetings.

"I understand that, Davien, but if I'm to present this information to the Earth government, I need details of what you've done. Who you've addressed. What you're prepared to give up. I would also imagine they will require you to choose either Earth citizenship or *Ba'Tuan.*"

The man before her opened his mouth, but she raised a hand. "I know. It doesn't seem right. I understand that you identify with both species, but should something happen to the agreement between our planets, you will be required to choose sides."

"But I can't! I'm both *Ba'Tuan* and human!" he screeched indignantly, and Dria tried again to soothe his ruffled sensitivities.

"Davien, if you were on *Dirustandi*, you'd be asked the same question."

"But that's archaic thinking!" He threw his hands in the air. "I shouldn't have to choose!" She sighed. "I understand your frustrations. But I need to present an argument to the government of Earth. If war broke out between our two species—" He opened his mouth, but she raised her hand, signaling him to stop. "Which side would you choose? I'd have to choose *Ba'Tuan*, because that's my homeworld and the one I feel the closest attachment to." The moment she uttered the words, she knew she'd made a tactical mistake.

Davien's lip curled and his gaze turned glacial. "So you'd choose them over us?" He reared back. "I'm wasting my time with you then. Excuse me, *Turana*."

God! Is this what my father has to deal with on a daily basis? I'd rather let my younger brother take over the position than to suffer this kind of intransigence! She leaned forward, ready to calm the situation, when a rumble began, growing louder and more insistent. The screaming of metal and the cracking of masonry was deafening.

Dria was instantly up and moving, her eyes tracking back and forth, searching for the threat. The thunderous noise continued, yet the walls stayed still and tall. She searched for and found Marcus's face. He too was clearly confused by the sounds of a distressed building, and he reached out, gripping her shoulders hard. There was comfort in the bite of his fingers in her flesh.

"We have to get out of here." The gravity in Marcus's tones ate at her.

"Yes. I'll get them out. You..." She didn't want to tell him to check the building, but they both knew he had to. They needed to know what was causing whatever was going on.

"I'll be careful. Just keep my people around you. We can't afford to take any chances with your safety."

What about yours? The cry rose from deep within, but she beat it back. He had a job to do, and so did she. Dria nodded slowly before rounding everyone up while Marcus and another of his team headed further inside the building.

She wanted to follow him, but the reality was, her people needed *her* assistance. *Her people.* The thought stilled her. *That sums it up, doesn't it?* She shook away the intrusion and set to work again.

She herded them out into the car park, but the whole time her gaze rested on the building. Her stomach jittered like a flight of butterflies taking to wing. Dria scrunched her hands together and waited.

When Marcus exited the community center, her heart started the low, steady thump against her ribs, the feeling she now associated with his proximity.

In his hand he carried a small amplifier, a tiny digital device, and on his face was a scowl. "It was a bloody trick!"

"*What?*" It seemed unbelievable that anyone would do this. "Who?"

He grimaced. "The Incubi." Marcus reached into his pocket and pulled out a crumpled piece of parchment coated with clear plasti-seal. He shoved it in her direction. "Read it."

This time is just a warning. Next time the repercussions will be far more wide ranging. Go home and take the hybrids with you.

"This can't be, surely?"

One look at his face told her they both knew the truth—the threat was very real.

"We have to get out of here. Now." Marcus gripped her hand and tugged.

Dria let him drag her away, realizing her continued presence put everyone in more danger.

Marcus shoved her into a car then got in the front seat, canted slightly so he could see the milling bystanders.

"We need to find them. Quickly. This fear cannot be condoned," she said.

His gaze speared her in the mirror of the vehicle. "We'll stop them. You and I together."

CHAPTER 9

arcus understood Dria's fury. The depths of her frustration at her inability to act gnawed at his gut.

Hours had passed and night fell. They'd eaten in front of their mini-comps as they worked, but no more information was revealed.

His fingers strayed to his head, and he dragged them through his hair as he eyed the large board they'd erected to hang their evidence on.

"Do you think that board will help us?" Her gaze settled on him.

"I read that in the past centuries many law enforcement officers used this system with excellent results." His eyes strayed to the collection of photos, information, and references.

"We're just missing one clue. The one that will tie this whole damned mess together." He stalked around the table. *At least there haven't been any more attacks since Dria arrived—or any where she's been the target.* There'd been three more attacks on hybrids though.

Each tagged *courtesy of the Incubi.*

Ding! The sound echoed in the near silence, and he spun. "What is it?"

"It's the analysis of the list of those who purchased the chemicals.

No one person has ordered enough to create the missile." She slumped down and he laid gentle hands on her shoulders.

"Maybe not, but if they had, it would almost be too simple." The supple skin beneath his touch felt rigid and he massaged gently.

"But until we can find a match, work out who is partnered with them, we don't have anything. By now..." Defeat threaded through her voice, and it infuriated him to hear how weary she sounded.

"Our people are looking for alternatives. I've got one working on fingerprint and DNA evidence. You have others working on tracking down known associates of Incubi and their sympathizers. We're both working through anything that occurs to us, and you're offering yourself up as a diversion. With limited resources—"

"It's not enough." She shoved back from the table, breathing hard, chest rising and falling in a rapid motion. His heart lurched in his chest. "We should have them by now!"

Unable to withstand the pain in her voice, he reached out and pulled her close, enfolding her in a hug. "We'll get them, Dria. We just need to be patient."

"I don't..."

"It'll be okay. *Shh...*" He rubbed circles over her back as she nestled in, her body tight against his, and when her hands wound around his waist and held on, his chest tightened, obstructing his breath.

"Marcus, I don't know what to do. I've always been in control of my own destiny. Able to negotiate whatever needs to be done, without leaning on anyone, but this time..." Her voice hitched as he dipped down, planning to offer only support. When she turned her face up to him, he swooped, pressing his lips against hers.

The only sound in the room now was their groans as they pushed closer together. *Ripe. Succulent.* The thoughts zoomed into his mind, then melted away as his body quaked. Urgent desire, the pressure in his groin, and the feel of her...

He jerked back, grasping a tiny thread of sanity. "God damn."

"Marcus?" She sounded uncertain, and he wanted to take back those two words that had clearly unsettled her.

He'd never felt like this before. He was both aroused and protective in equal measure. It added a whole new dimension, and one he wasn't sure was easy to deal with.

"You don't want—" she whispered, the sound broken and forlorn.

"I want you so badly I'm aching with it. Dria, if you want me, then put me out of my misery. Tell me."

One second then another passed, and the tiny hope shivered like a flame before disappearing. He turned, hoping he could somehow assuage the need that roared in his veins.

"Don't turn away, Marcus. I...I want you too."

His turn was executed with lightning speed, his gaze zeroing in on her face. "Be sure, Dria. Once we take this step, there can be no going back."

She reached up, cupping his chin, and electricity zinged through his body. Her soft smile turned his insides to mush. "I have no intention of changing my mind." Then she kissed him.

*H*er entire body ached with hunger. Her brain struggled to get past the swirling vortex of emotions contained in his skin-burning kiss. Heat filled her as he clasped her shoulders.

I need more!

Her fingers strayed from his chin to his chest, where they found the buttons on his shirt. She'd watched him all day, aware of the highly defined muscles hidden beneath the cotton. The memory of him the other night haunted her dreams.

Pop! The buttons hit the floor as she jerked his shirt open. Her fingers rested against his chest for a moment, then she pulled back with a hiss as she caressed his taut muscles.

So perfect!

"I'm not sure I can manage a lot of foreplay this time, Marcus. I want you so badly, my knees are knocking together."

His rumble of laughter echoed in her bones as his hands slid to the hidden fasteners of her dress. "That's good, because I'm too damned hungry for you right now."

The chiffon floated to the floor, leaving her covered only by lacy underwear. *Thank goodness...* The thought petered away as he brushed the tiny straps down, leaving her bra gaping. As Dria started to remove the last barely-there wisps of material, he stilled her trembling fingers.

"So beautiful." He spoke unevenly as if overcome with the same emotions that wavered within her. "All mine."

Their lips collided, moving hungrily together. He thrust his tongue inside her mouth, and she couldn't stop a moan from erupting. His hands skated over her belly, then brushed the underside of her breasts before sliding behind her. Her breasts sagged as he released her bra strap.

Dria hurried, searching for the buckle of his belt, then tugged at his pants impatiently.

With a thud, the material fell to the floor.

Marcus pulled away. "Last chance." The whisper of his breath caressed her skin.

"Don't need one." She took a step back and hooked her thumbs in the side of her panties.

Dria captured his gaze as she slid them all the way down her legs.

His gaze turned molten, and she was sure her bones would melt.

She trembled as Marcus stepped toward the door, latching it slowly. The sound echoed in the quiet night. Turning, Marcus shucked his underwear, and she noted just how aroused he was.

She reached out, her touch gliding over his chest. *Warm and lightly bronzed.* "You're...*amazing!*"

He laughed and the rumble ricocheted through her. "That's supposed to be my line."

Her eyes drooped to half-mast as they came together, lips and tongues tangling while hands grasped flesh and kneaded. She shivered as he nibbled his way down the column of her neck, and she stretched, unable to contain her breathless reaction. "Oh God, that feels so good." At her collarbone he stilled and dipped his tongue in the tiny depression where neck met shoulder.

"Your skin's so silky soft." Then he nuzzled and she groaned, hoping he'd continue. The molten pool of heat in her belly sent fire licking through every inch of her body.

Gently, Marcus cupped both her breasts and held them up, before dipping down to kiss one nipple then the other. As his breath teased the distended nubs they engorged further. "Marcus, I need you now! Please!" she whispered hoarsely into the night air, and reached for his hips. "Come to me. Fill me."

As if waiting for her invitation, he dragged her closer, drawing every inch of her front against his. Wild sensations drove rational thought from her mind as nerves sizzled.

His cock, hard and urgent, nestled at her most intimate curls. She widened her stance, and when his tip slid against her clitoris she gasped, digging her fingers into his shoulders.

His fingers grasped her bottom and raised her, pushed her to the table behind her. As she rose, her bottom slid over the wood.

Then he plunged. *Deep. Hard.*

"God help me!" The words ground out of him, but she didn't care as the sensation of fullness ratcheted her arousal higher.

He moved, a subtle shift that rocked her all the way to the depths of her soul. Again he thrust, and the electric sensations zoomed down her veins, so every inch of her body gloried in his taking.

Slam! Slam! Marcus ground against her, each action harder and more urgent than the last. A cataclysmic reaction began in her belly and between her legs. Her engorged breasts moved pendulously against his hard pectoral muscles. She struggled to breathe as they moved together, seeking their mutual release.

Deep within, an invisible wire quivered then snapped, releasing her powerful orgasm until nothing existed but overwhelming pleasure.

Fingers speared into her flesh as she came back to her senses and the sensation of his body releasing deep within her. She held him, her body limp as he drooped against her.

Their panting breaths mingled with the musky scent of sex.

What have I...

"Dria, I was on you like some kind of rutting bull!"

She nearly laughed at the disgust in his voice. "That's okay, Marcus. I wasn't exactly ladylike either."

They both laughed, a tired echo.

"We should..." They spoke in unison, then broke off, averting their gazes.

Now that the act was over, some of her initial inhibitions returned, and she nearly covered her breasts before the knowledge he'd done more than look at them battered her.

"I should retire." It was the best she could do, but a trace of hurt slipped over his face before disappearing.

"Yes. That's probably best." He turned, and the action cut her to the quick.

"Will you..." Dria licked her lips, realizing she wanted him beside her. Not just for sex, but the companionship she'd experienced since being with him. "Will you join me?"

She held herself still, and waited.

He slowly turned back to her, and for an instant she was sure he'd refuse. Instead, he held out a hand. "I'd be honored."

*M*arcus turned his head as he opened his eyes. *This isn't my bed.*

Warmth invaded his body, and he instantly knew where he was. *Dria.*

They'd shared more than just their bodies. Now they shared a bed and an intimacy that he wanted to shy away from.

He itched to reach out and touch her, but he held back, unsure of himself. Could he trust any of the emotions that roiled in his belly? He'd been wrong before. The sound of her breath, the quiet exhalation, soothed the passion that burned him.

With care he rolled back, flinging an arm over his eyes. Not since

Christina had he wanted a woman like this. Even now, his morning erection made itself known and he wanted nothing more than to roll her over and thrust deeply within her body.

What the hell was he going to do? A sense of unreality swept over him. She was a bloody *princess*! *From another planet.* How the *hell* had he managed to forget that?

She moved and her hand snaked across his belly. "Uh... Marcus?" She sounded groggy but also happy.

He slid his hand over hers. "Right here." His gut rattled as nerves assailed him. "You don't have any second thoughts, do you? Because I don't."

He closed his burning eyes at her careful words. She'd summed up exactly the turmoil he faced. "This can't be long term, Dria. You'll go home to *Dirustandi* and—"

"Actually, I'm not so sure I will. While I've been here, I've done some serious soul searching. It could be that what I'm thinking will impact on my current status."

Marcus rolled to his side and gazed deeply into her eyes. "What do you mean?" She shook her head, clearly confused as her brow furrowed. "As the *Turana*, I'm

supposed to take over from my father. I'm the first born, but the pomp and circumstance of reigning isn't me. Never was. My brother Lora, he's more inclined to that. Until now I blindly accepted the future mapped out for me. I'm wondering if perhaps..." She shrugged. "Before I can start sorting that out though, we need to find and neutralize the Incubi."

"You still have to return to *Dirustandi*. It's your home."

Dria bit her lip. "When I was talking to the hybrids, I had to ask them where their loyalties lay. I told one of them that for me, it was the *Ba'Tua*, but that was... My thinking was simplistic. I'm both human and *Ba'Tuan*. What I've experienced with you..."

Her words stole the oxygen from his lungs. "But it's your home."

"Yes, it is, but I've learned that a person can mean more than a planet. I'll always be *Ba'Tuan*, but I've also realized I can be human at the same time. It's confusing but..."

He leaned in and kissed her, a gentle brush of lips. Dria wasn't promising him forever or to stay by his side. But clearly she was rethinking her path in life, and if that let him spend more time with her, then he'd take whatever she offered.

He shook his head on a sigh. The working day awaited. "We should get up."

"You're already *up!*" She laughed playfully, and his eyes widened in surprise. This was a side of her he hadn't seen before.

"I meant out of bed." He shoved the covers aside and snorted at her. *Shame about that.* He grabbed the clothes he'd hastily collected last night and tugged them on. "I'm going to shower and change, then we can meet for breakfast."

"Hang on, Marcus."

He turned back to face her as she hurried toward him and rose up on her tiptoes. "Good morning to you too."

Her kiss wasn't a peck—it scorched him thoroughly as she massaged his lips with hers. They were firm and possessive, and his entire body reacted. When he opened to her with a moan she sipped at his tongue, every movement an erotic statement of ownership. One he welcomed.

Finally, Dria pulled away, her skin a rosy shade of pink and her nipples strawberry buds of sensual delight. "That should keep you going until later."

Then she turned away and favored him with a view of her dimpled buttocks. His groin tightened further, but he retreated to his own room. He had some thinking and planning to do, and while a naked Dria cavorted in front of him, all he could concentrate on was her.

CHAPTER 10

ria let the water course over her naked and very aroused body. She wished Marcus had stayed, but of course, he was right. They both had things to do.

Her body continued to pulse but the urgency had drained away. Dria ignored it as best she could, until the rasp of the loofah over her breasts created a delightful friction. "Oooh..." Excitement welled again and she hissed.

She braced both hands on the wall of the shower, dropped her head forward, and breathed deeply as she ignored the hunger. It didn't work.

"Drop water temperature fifteen degrees."

The temperature drop left her shivering, but achieved the result she was seeking. Dria searched for focus as she exhaled.

"Need to track down the buyers. Follow them back to any associates. There must be something." But so far, they hadn't found anything. Why? What were they missing?

"Water off." She stepped from the stall, reached for the towel hanging on the rail, and wiped the droplets from her body.

The light on the screen switched on and off, capturing her attention. Dria reached for the mini-comp.

"Matches found," the disembodied voice of the computer echoed.

"Thank you!" She snatched it up and headed for the door, ready to show Marcus, when she realized she was still naked. "Oh, you have to be kidding me."

Dria quickly authorized a backup as she donned clothing. A pale pair of pants and lightweight blouse were lying over the back of the chair, ready for her to wear to today's official engagements. She'd rather climb into her exercise clothing, but this was the first to hand. She shoved her feet into pumps and headed for the door, scooping up the mini-comp as she moved.

The door opened without a sound and she slipped through.

In the corridor, Simpson, one of Marcus's many assistants waited. "Can I be of service, *Turana*?"

"Oh, yes. I'm looking for the commander. I've received important information that will hopefully help us conclude this mission."

Simpson's face changed. In an instant it morphed from young and guileless to twisted and angry.

Dria couldn't help herself. She backed up. "*Simpson?*"

"You're too damned clever for your own good. All we needed was another few days, and we'd have finally managed to destroy the Accord." The guileless look returned. "You're going for a visit, *Turana*." He slapped a transmitter to her shirt, and while she tried to remove it, he tugged a tiny remote from his pocket and depressed the button with a smile.

"*Marcus!*" Even as she screamed, the world turned black.

The tiny tracker app Marcus had downloaded to his chrono blared.

"Dria!" He shoved back from the table and through the door, his feet pounding on the tiled floor as he headed to her room. "Dria? Dammit, answer me."

If the app on his chrono was right though, she was gone. He'd set it to alert him to a transmission. *Gone!* He searched her rooms while his heartrate spiked.

He tugged the mini-comp from his pocket as his mind worked through how this could have happened. He called up the location of all his people. Everyone was accounted for except...

Simpson?

In his mind, a vision of the young, dark-haired man who'd been delivering meals and running errands rose. "Dammit."

Sick... That tugged at his memory and he contacted his cousin Arends, the one who'd been unavailable. "Simon? Can you talk?"

"Hey, Marcus. Sure. What's up?"

"You were sick at the beginning of the mission. Did they ever find out what was wrong with you?"

"Oh, it was food poisoning. My morning yogurt contained some kind of bacteria. Did you miss the safety recall?" There was amusement in his cousin's voice, but a yawing pit opened in the bottom of Marcus's belly.

"Are you available?" He needed him as part of his crew now, if they were to find Dria.

His gut roiled. They needed to work swiftly.

"Sure."

"Good. Transport to my quarters immediately." He broke off the call and swiftly sent out an urgent summons to the rest of his team.

One by one they checked in. It was only minutes, but felt like a lifetime. "The Incubi have the *Turana*. It appears Simpson, who replaced Simon, was a plant."

"Simpson? He's... He was a new transfer in about two months ago!" Simon frowned. "I don't know where he came from."

Marcus turned to the young blond man. "Find out everything you can about him." Another thought struck. Dria complaining her yogurt tasted sour and was unwell. On the side in the dining room was the breakfast set up on a tray. "And get that yogurt analyzed."

Simon nodded and started moving.

A young female ensign, a specialist in computational assessment, looked up. "I've found her signature, Vane." Her face was pale and tight. "It's in a remote area, in the hinterland."

"Get me the details. We need to move quickly."

The woman nodded and set to work.

"Gear up, everyone. We're going in to get the *Turana*."

*D*ria fumed and worked feverishly at the bonds behind her back. *Damn them to the seven hells and back!*

How in the world had Simpson got past Marcus's stringent safety protocols? She knew Marcus had been concerned enough that he'd arranged for her to be placed in the barracks after the situation at the hotel.

The room where her captors had stashed her had a view of the mountains and foliage outside. She grimaced, knowing that even if she got away, she didn't have a clue as to where she was or where to go.

Hell, she didn't even know which continent she was on. Who knew what human transmitters were capable of? After all, they'd had access to the *Ba'Tuan* technology for nearly a quarter of a century. Did they have geographic limitations like theirs?

Each tug at her bonds tore at her skin, but she remained quiet while she worked.

The door opened, and she stilled. "Where am I, and why did you take me?" The questions were rhetorical. The first one wouldn't be answered and the second was merely textbook.

She needed to keep them from inspecting the ties at her back, otherwise they'd know she was almost free.

"*Turana*, glad to finally meet you. Our Simpson did his work quite well and followed my instructions."

Dria frowned at the woman who took a seat in the chair in front of her. She was likely in her sixth decade, but well preserved with immaculate hair and carefully applied cosmetics.

"You're here because you represent the *Ba'Tua*. We would have preferred scaring you off, but you're more than you appear. You were supposed to have been a silly piece of royal fluff with more hair than brains. Sadly, you've brought this on yourself as you involved yourself in human politics." The woman looked down and observed her nails.

"Who are you?"

She gazed up at Dria and smiled. "Oh, so they never told you about me. Your mother and that bloody Cedun. My name is Felicity Kensington-Mare. You can call me Floss. That's how your mother knows me." She smiled broadly, and it was cold. Full of menace.

Floss? The name didn't ring a bell, but that didn't mean anything, did it? "Why do you want the human and *Ba'Tuan* Accord to fail? Our combined strength—"

"Oh, stop chattering at me. You're not as dumb as you make out. Surely you know? My lover was your mother's partner for years. He wasn't human or *Ba'Tuan*." The final words were triumphant, and a glimmer of amusement filled her eyes.

Dria's belly cramped. The *Galecian*? "You aren't one of them?"

"Oh no. They weren't really interested in me when they came to retrieve Garret, but I offered them a deal. Something far more...long term. I offered to destroy the agreement between the humans and *Ba'Tuans* if they would in turn give me supplies. Oh, and I demanded revenge on your mother. Anything I want they give me because they want Earth to join their alliance."

A chill invaded Dria's body. The *Galecians* weren't a species to form any kind of alliance with. They invaded, took slaves, and killed indiscriminately. A quick glance in Floss's direction told her there was no way the woman would listen rationally to anything she had to say on the matter.

Still, Dria needed to make one final attempt. "Look, Floss. Let me help you. You let me go and—"

The woman barked out a laugh—menacing and deep. For the first time Dria felt fear for herself.

"Dear, no matter what you do, the *Galecians* and I will rid Earth of the *Ba'Tuan* plague. Now, make yourself comfortable. They'll be here soon for you." With that, Floss rose and left her alone.

Hurry up, Marcus. Otherwise I'm in deep trouble.

CHAPTER 11

They transmitted to the location they'd chosen and Marcus cursed as a frond hit him in the face.

"Where the hell are we?" His furious snarl left several men recoiling.

"Sir, we're less than a kilometer from the *Turana's* location. By my calculations, we need to head over this rise and in the middle of the valley we'll find wherever she's being held. Marcus grunted and checked his stingray-450 semi-automatic rifle. After a week of urban fieldwork it felt odd in his hand—clumsy and unwieldy. He checked the terrain before striding out. The rest of his team would follow.

The ground beneath his feet crunched, and he silently cursed. It didn't help that his mind told him to slow down and plan, while his heart screamed there was little time left.

They moved as swiftly as possible, but took more care and attention as they ascended the ridge. At the top, he dragged field glasses from his utility belt. Nestled within the trees was a small house.

With swift movements, he silently organized his team. Three would head to the back of the property once he'd signaled it was safe. He and three others would take the main entrance.

Disquiet filled him. Where were the guards that should be

posted? The Incubi had successfully caused urban chaos, but here, there should be at least five or more guards posted. None of this made sense to him. It seemed like they didn't realize the gravity of the situation should they be detected. Or was there more?

He signaled for the group to advance, and he realized the building was more like a multi-roomed hut. Decrepit with shingles in need of replacing.

At the edge of the treeline, they stilled and Marcus waited, hidden by a tree fern. *No movement. Odd.*

Two grotty windows flanked the front door. Four small steps and a broken handrail led to the front door he wanted to avoid, at least until he knew he wasn't endangering Dria by entering. The windows had no curtains, so he'd need to be careful peering in. He needed to know exactly where they'd stashed Dria before entering the cottage.

The thumping of his heart crashed in his chest.

One click of his comm unit told them he was going in alone.

He advanced slowly, his eyes moving left and right. A bird in the distance screeched and took flight, and Marcus stilled. Waited.

The building was less than ten meters now and he dashed toward it, careful to scoot along the outer walls in silence.

He waited, letting his breathing settle.

Which window to check first? The door canted slightly to the left. It followed logic that the main room, then, was to the left. He'd be better to try the right first.

Marcus hugged the wall, sliding slowly until he was beneath the window. He turned and reached up, ensuring he remained at the very corner, then peered within.

The sight before him was chilling. There was Dria, tied to the wall.

He watched for a moment as she twisted and turned. As if some connection between them alerted her, she looked up and caught sight of him.

He lifted a finger to his lips and indicated he intended to raise the window. She glanced at the door in unspoken warning.

At his nod she stilled and some of the concern on her face melted away.

He slipped the rifle over his shoulder and braced himself, pushing against the wood. It moved a little way, then stilled. With a small grunt he slid the fingers of one hand then the other below the partly raised slider and tried again. It moved a little further, but not enough to let him in.

He peered at the sides, looking for an obstruction. Nothing. Maybe there was a stopper on the edge?

Taking the weight on one side, he slid his arm in and twisted enough to feel around. Sure enough something obstructed his way. Carefully, he gripped the panel of wood and removed it.

Now the window opened and he climbed within.

Dria gave one last jerk and freed herself. "Took you a while to get here."

He nearly laughed with joy. Instead, he released a whoosh of air from his lungs. Leaning forward, he whispered against her neck. "We need to be quick."

Her nod acknowledged his words. She too kept her voice low. "The ringleader is Floss. She knew my parents before they married, and she's the head of the Incubi. They're in league with the *Galecians*."

He'd heard the term *Galecian* before but couldn't place it. "Who are—"

"We don't have time for this. They're on their way, and we have to get out of here." Dria shoved against him, pushing him back the way he came.

Confusion filled him. Up until now, fear hadn't been something that Dria had exhibited.

Clearly the *Galecians* put the wind up her.

"Dria, where are the Incubi?"

She shook her head. "We don't have time to find them. Just get us out of here." She stumbled to the window and started to climb out just as a roar emanated from overhead.

The roar told her time was up. The *Galecians* had arrived. The cold, hard pit that formed in her belly when Floss had told her about her agreement became stone-like.

"We're too late. How many men do you have?" She reached out and grasped Marcus's shirt, twisting it in her hand.

"Another six. Why? Who is that, and what the hell was that noise?"

Before Dria could answer, the door burst open and Floss entered, her eyes wild. "What..." She stopped at the entrance, taking in the sight of Marcus.

In seconds, Floss recovered and whipped a tiny laser pistol from her pocket. Dria watched the woman as she considered their situation.

Two of us. Floss with a gun. Galecian ship overhead. The odds were bad. In fact, they were horrific.

"You have to let us go, Floss. If the *Galecians* get what they want, all humans will be little more than slaves. That's not what you want, is it?"

Floss ignored her concerns.

Her words were useless, and the sensation of failure filled her. They were going to die. Her mind emptied of everything except fear for herself, but more so, for Marcus. The truth stunned her. *I can't let the man I love die!*

She felt responsible that he was mixed up in all this. How could this happen? His experience was in dealing with humans, not *Galecians*. They were a totally different kettle of fish. *If I don't do something now, everything will be lost.* The thought freed her from the fear-induced paralysis.

"You have to let us go." She leaned forward, mentally calculating the distance between herself and the other woman.

Dria balanced on the balls of her feet, ready to move when Marcus did. He rushed the woman, fast as lightning. Even as Floss turned and fired, the door burst open again and three *Galecians* entered. Marcus wavered, a flash of red appearing on his clothes, then he slumped to the floor.

"*Nooooo!*" Dria swept around, leg raised to attack Floss. The sound of her foot against Floss's leg made a thwacking noise. The tiny weapon fell to the floor, and Dria dove for it. Her hand clasped it and she turned, rising up.

"Wait, *Turana!*" The lead *Galecian* raised both hands in an attitude of treaty.

Dria panted and waited. "Leave him alone!" She waved the weapon from side to side, unsure which currently was the bigger threat, her mind scrambled by the knowledge that Marcus was hurt.

The officer turned to her, then pointed at Marcus who groaned. "He's injured, but it's not life threatening. Should I offer medical assistance, Gurdu?"

The leader, Gurdu, looked in her direction. "Yes. Have Manteru take the female human into custody."

"What?" What the hell was going on? Dria shook her head. "What are you doing here? Earth is a protected planet under the Callistan Agreement. *Galecia* has no business here." Her voice wobbled, and she silently acknowledged her words were full of bravado.

Marcus was injured, *Galecians* were there with weapons, and there were maybe six other humans somewhere out there. *Why weren't they in here?*

The whine of a transmitter filled the air, and a tactical guardian from her own planet appeared before her. The gold and yellow of his uniform and the purple pips told her of his position as Commander. "*Turana*, we're here on your father's orders."

The gun she'd been holding slid to the floor with a thud. "My father's orders?"

Joruzan, her step-grandfather, materialized beside her. "Commander, Ist'an, *Turana*. I see all is..." His voice broke off, and his gaze locked on Marcus. The one who'd first advanced had knelt beside him and was already cutting away the material from his wound site.

"Would someone please explain what the hell is going on?" She looked at Joruzan. "You, Joruzan. Explain to me what is happening."

"Your father and the *Galecian*, Ran'uzan, created a political alliance three years ago. When the ruler, Amu'zan, passed on. Emperoer Ran'uzan became the next in line to the throne, after Emperor Vil'nak. Emporer Vil'nak died two days ago. Ran'uzan immediately enacted a treaty and sent Gurdu, his second, to deal with this situation. He'd been aware that there were factions that coveted Earth. Ran'uzan neutralized them and wants to enter into treaty negotiations. Their power base has dwindled with Vil'nak's desire to colonize and has left them open to attack."

Dria looked at the man she'd known for so long. "But why wasn't I informed about..."

Joruzan smiled enigmatically. "Until now, you didn't need to know."

Anger coursed, scalding her. "So instead you sent me here, put lives at risk—"

"That's enough, Dria! This is neither the time nor the location for such a discussion. You will be recalled soon to discuss this with your father. Until then, you will hunt out the rest of the Incubi and deal with them." He dismissed her by turning his back. "Thank you for your assistance Gurdu. The *Turaa* will, of course, require your report, as no doubt will your leader."

"If you are ready, Ist'an?" The leader spoke to the one treating Marcus, who was now sitting upright, his face tight but the bleeding diminished.

"Yes, sir." Ist'an gave a tight bow, then he and his people disappeared.

With an angry look in Joruzan's direction, Dria moved to Marcus and crouched down. "Are you okay?"

His gaze was distant, but he was alive. "I've felt better."

She lifted a shaking hand to his face. "I'll bet. Let's go home."

He nodded, panting heavily. She wanted him out of there. "You have a transmitter?" "Yeah. Two in my pocket—one for you and one for me."

She removed them from his pocket, wincing as he groaned his discomfort.

"I'll alert your team," she said. "And then we can—"

Bang! Crash! The door thudded open and Marcus's people hurried in. Looks of disbelief flooded their faces as they took in the tableau.

Dria looked up. "He's fine. But we're going home. Joruzan, you can sort this mess out." With that she depressed the buttons and the room turned black.

EPILOGUE

The sun shone down as Dria left the palace. Her parents had been stunned at the ultimatum she'd just given them. Down below the mountain, in a small cafe, Marcus waited for her.

For Marcus, she'd concocted a story about needing to return home and that her parents wished to meet him. Today wasn't the time though. No, she needed the truth about Christina before taking a chance. Dria had reached the point of no return in the small shack when Marcus had been hurt. Like a lightning strike, it had hit her—he was the most important thing in her life.

Her fingers shook as she transmitted to the cafe door. Peering in, she glanced around for him.

He looked as nervous as she felt. Dria fussed with the collar of her gown before stepping forward. If she could somehow encourage him to open up, then she could make the most important declaration of her life.

Marcus turned his eyes to her as she walked in his direction. "Everything done?"

She smiled. "Yes. Let's sit down."

He smiled tightly. "I already am."

The idiocy of her suggestion left her feeling more on edge than before as she tugged on a seat and lowered herself into the chair.

"I'd like to talk to you about...stuff." She almost groaned, realizing how lame the word sounded, but right now, all the careful rehearsal of what she meant to say eluded her.

"Good. I'd like... There's something I'd like to discuss with you." His grin wobbled, and she leaned forward. "I need to tell you about Christina."

Now it was Dria's turn to struggle with her smile. "Okay."

"Christina was... I met her on one of my missions. She was involved with the drug underground. My job was to extract as much information as I could from her. She had figured out who I was. Of course, that helped her achieve her ultimate aim. At the end, once she had the information she needed, she packed up her stuff, then decided she should tell me goodbye in person. Unknown to all of us, the cartel set explosives. Since the explosion, I've blamed myself because she waited to talk to me, as if it were somehow my fault that she was killed. Once the contents of her vehicle were listed I knew she had been planning on leaving me, but I held onto my grief and let it rule my life. I let her lies color my views on relationships and stopped trusting in what I could have."

Dria rubbed her forehead, struggling to understand what he was saying.

"Did you love her?" The words were dragged from the deepest recess of her soul. He shook his head. "I thought I did. But I didn't know what love was. Not then."

She tilted her head in his direction. He scrubbed his hand over his face, and the action left her feeling unbalanced.

"Marcus..."

"Shhh." He stopped her words as he touched a fingertip against her lips. "Let me finish." She nodded and kept her eyes locked on his face, entranced as he slipped from the chair and dropped to one knee. "I'm really not worthy of you. You're a princess, and I'm a mere warrior. But I love you like no one else ever will. I love your passion and drive. I adore everything about you. Please consider finding a way to—"

Her eyes burned as she dropped to her knees in front of him. "Marcus. I love you too. I have since... I don't really know when. I've just informed my parents I cannot continue as *Turana*. It's not who I'm meant to be. My life... It's with you. If you'll have me?"

She waited but the seconds dragged like minutes. Then he wound his arms around her waist and pulled her close.

"You're everything to me. When you were taken prisoner... I couldn't function. It was like the other half of me was...gone. We can marry and stay here if you want?"

She shook her head. "Marry, yes, but not stay here. I've asked my parents to grant me the position of Ambassador to Earth. I can do more good there. There's plenty to keep me busy, and to be honest, the little bit I saw of Earth... I liked it."

He kissed her. Hard. She allowed it for a brief moment, then pulled away.

"As lovely as this is, I have one more surprise." She lifted her transmitter, and a grin snaked over her face.

His eyes sparkled with excitement, and she felt herself leaning forward, while his lips formed one word. "Where?"

"Somewhere infinitely more private." With a laugh, she depressed the button, and hand in hand the world turned black.

Did you enjoy this book by Imogene Nix?
There's more on the following pages. Just keep turning to see what else.

THE CELTIC CUPID TRILOGY

When Cupid—otherwise known as Diocail— is banished from his home on a remote Scottish Island, he's set a series of tasks by the great god Lugh, who also happens to be his father.

In **Blame The Wine**, he must bring two lovers together... BBW Cara and James, the man she's lusted over from afar who happens to be a super geek and head Veha Industries.

In *A Stranger's Embrace*, Diocail is driven to help an emotionally fragile Jane and Davis, a famous author. The task is more complicated, with the existence of Carstairs her could-be ex-husband and teenage daughter, Frannie.

In *Revenge on Cupid,* Diocail must take the ultimate chance and find his own happily ever after with Simone. Sometimes the past gets in the way and HEA's don't come cheap though.

The dusty, dingy little diner was full, even with its current state of cleanliness—or lack thereof. People from the surrounding offices didn't care about anything except the incredible, well-prepared food at a reasonable cost. They flooded in, like waves to the shore. As one tide left, another swept in.

"Honestly, Simone. I'm going to try getting his attention one more time. If that doesn't work, I'm out of there. I mean, how long can I keep trying?" Cara picked at the caramel tart she hadn't been able to resist with the cheap metal fork and flicked the blob of fresh cream that sat on top to the side of the plate.

"You've said that tons of times before. Besides, what are you going to do to get his attention? Hmm? Walk naked through the typing pool?" Simone bobbed the straw in her smoothie as she eyed her friend with a frown. "It's been what? Eighteen months since you saw him, and you've mooned over him from a distance ever since you met him. You need to move on, Cara. That is, unless there's something you haven't shared?"

The query was arch. Cara shivered even as she shook her head. "No."

Simone quirked an eyebrow, obviously unconvinced with the answer. Cara let out a deep sigh of frustration. "There's a position...it's only temporary, for a PA reporting directly to him." She speared a forkful of tart, chewed quickly and swallowed, before continuing. "In his office, full-time for the period of the engagement. I saw the memo yesterday. I mean, I have the skills, right? I can type, answer phones, make coffee, file, greet people. What's more, I can probably do it better than all those size eights in the typing pool that Ms. Jackman seems to prefer." She nodded thoughtfully. "All I have to do is get past the ogre in Human Resources."

Simone stared at her, disbelief clear on her face. "Girl, I so remember that woman. If you think you can get past her, you're doing better than I ever did. That's why I left Veha Industries, remember? Maybe it's time to haul out your resumé and consider some other options. Look for something better." Simone shook her head and billows of her crimson hair swirled through the still air.

Cara understood Simone only had her best interests at heart. But this time she knew the outcome would be different. Hell, she could feel it in the air. The tingle of expectation.

"Cara, the HR ogre will hang you out for breakfast before she offers you anything like a position in that office. Remember her mantra? Good looks and good work make for a positive workplace!"

Simone didn't sugar-coat anything. It was another great reason for their long- term friendship. Honesty. But Cara didn't want to hear the truth in the statement. Even if it was exactly as her friend said.

Cara nodded quickly. "Yeah, I know, but if I don't try, then I won't know how close I can get to him, right? And the only way to catch his attention is to get past *her* and see him in person." Cara quaked a little at the information she needed to share. The favor she needed to ask. "Anyway, I tidied up my resumé and dropped the application into a memo envelope yesterday, so it's too late to back out now. I mean, fortune favors the brave. Doesn't it? If I don't snag an interview, I'm going to visit the career advisor across the street and register with them." She shrugged. "I'll look for temp work until something more long-term shows up. I can see what they have on offer and well...who knows? Maybe a job with the right boss is just waiting for me. But I'd rather this worked out, to be honest." Her voice trailed off into a whisper. "I really wish he would notice me."

Simone took a long slurp of her banana drink, and Cara noticed her questioning gaze even as she squirmed. Finally, Simone nodded. "It's your funeral. So anyway, you'd better show me this memo if you want me to be a referee for you. I'm guessing that's what you need, right? I'll have to know what I'm supposed to say about you before they ring."

Cara smiled. "Thanks, Simone. I knew I could count on you." She slipped a piece of paper out of her handbag and handed it over. "Sorry it's a bit creased. It was in the bottom of my bag, I stashed it so none of the others from the pool would see. You know how it is."

Available from Love Books Publishing
books2read.com/CelticCupid

Direct Autographed Copy
http://bit.ly/2vs7wtS

STAR OF ISHTAR

Warriors of the Elector
Book One

The first time Elara laid eyes on Grayson was when he rescued her from the clutches of a madman and his scientists who were kidnapping humans and conducting horrific experiments on them. That was years ago. In spite of her attempts to deepen their relationship, they remained nothing more than close friends.Now Elara is a medic with the Admiralty, and she knows what she wants. It's been Grayson since the beginning. When Elara is stationed on the *Star of Ishtar*, she arrives with a plan to further her career. But this time her plan has an added bonus—to finally get her man.

Grayson's spent years fighting the connection between himself and Elara. He's certain it only exist because he saved her life. But his will is failing, and he fears he just might give in to temptation.

———————————————

"I finally made it." Elara Sudonne watched as the hull of the *Star of Ishtar* loomed in the inky darkness. She clutched her hands tightly together as the shuttle approached the hulking battleship.

This would be her new home and first combat ST placement for the Earth Empire. She quaked inwardly with nerves but fought to keep her serene exterior. Previously her deployments had consisted solely of on-planet expeditions and in rehabilitation and dirtside facilities. When the chance had arisen to move to the battleship, she'd grabbed it with both hands.

The frigid air chilled her bones as she sat in her shuttle seat, but a trickle of sweat inched its way down her back under the fresh gray wool flight uniform. Little puffs of vapor escaped her mouth as she rubbed her arms. Nerves stretched tight, she looked through the small portal at the front of the vessel. She wanted to tug at the collar that somehow seemed to have grown tighter as the ship loomed ahead, but instead she firmed her mouth, straightened her spine, and concentrated on the future.

"So damned long." She'd been working toward this outcome since the day Grayson Myatt and Duvall McCord had saved her from her Ru'Edan captors. She was lucky, she'd survived the 'experimenta-tion' of the Ru'Edan leader Crick Sur Banden's scientists. "And all I have to remind me are my scars." She didn't grin at her own joke.

The person seated behind her jostled but she ignored it, lost in her memories. On that day, so very long ago, the young Elara, fresh-faced and with idealistic views of the empire, was taken from the mall where she'd been shopping with friends, thrust into the back of a transport vehicle, and given to the Ru'Edan scientists to experiment on.

For days they'd worked on her and others, seeking an average pain threshold of humans, slicing her skin then noting reactions and how long it took to heal. They'd cut her arms, body, and even her face, and now she carried the extensive scarring of the exercise as a reminder to herself and others of what they were fighting for. Freedom. The freedom of Earth and its allied planets.

She'd never relinquished hope, it had been her constant companion as she fought against the all-consuming terror. Then they'd found her in that dirty, disused warehouse. They'd found others too, in various states of death and decay. The smells of despair had filled the air with a fetid ripeness that she'd never been able to forget.

Since that day she'd promised herself that she would pay the Ru'Edan back for what they'd done to her. What they'd taken from her. Over the years, she tempered and honed the rage while remaining adamant that she would see the final act played out. She couldn't physically fight, but she had learned about trauma, knew it and understood how it affected a person, and used it as a weapon.

The iron will forged through her experiences had fed her determination, and she'd applied herself to study, finishing in the top ten percent of her class. She entered the medical program at the academy, working hard to excel. Her family remained supportive if perplexed as to why she had chosen to keep reminding herself of what had happened.

The maw of the *Star of Ishtar* loomed closer, opening its cavernous mouth as she watched through the portal. She could hear the voices of the shuttle crew signaling their intention to enter and land, the tinny confirmation coming swiftly. She watched avidly while the shuttle maneuvered, imagining the invisible shields dropping to allow it entry.

Her hands twisted with fear and anger, but she tamped down her emotions. Anger never helped anyone. Staying strong, knowing your history, and ensuring it couldn't be repeated, they were the answers, she told herself firmly, pulling herself from the grip of a dark past so horrific she still saw it in her dreams. She pushed it away to the recesses of her mind and focused on what she was about to do.

A squark overhead, the usual mechanical sound that alerted all on board to a transmission by the captain, caught her attention. "Attention all passengers. We are entering the shuttle bay. Please ensure when you disembark you remove all personal items. Move beyond the white line and wait for your designation."

The lights of the bay flashed as they entered, and once again Elara marveled at how far humanity had moved since they had first walked the Earth. She saw the opening of the structure as the shuttle moved into the bay, inching forward slowly until it stopped its ponderous motion and began its descent to the floor. Something deep inside warmed even as the shuttle's environmental systems began to synchronize with the cooler temperature of the *Star of Ishtar*, and she felt a smile crawl its way over her face.

Elara breathed in deeply, inhaling the metallic-tasting, recycled air and welcoming the calmness that settled on her body. Her eyes closed as she filled her lungs. "I'm here." There was more than a little satisfaction in her tone, and she smiled. She slowly exhaled, finding that center of peace she relied on.

A loud thud and clank echoed as the deep drone split the air. The engines were powering down, and there she was, on one of the Earth Empire's Emeritus class battleships. She sat in her seat, waiting for the all clear from the captain, and once it sounded through the cabin, she rose, tugging at the webbing belt and disengaging it.

The small backpack beside her was all she carried as she made her way to the exit, not needing to duck as so many others did. She stepped through the door, her hands gripping the rail of the cold, metal stairs which connected to the side of the gray shuttle.

She clambered down them slowly, savoring the experience. The sting of the cold on her hands from the stairs, frigid from even their brief exposure to the blackness of space, made her flinch inwardly.

The shuttle journey from the Admiralty's strategic base at Aenna to their current position had taken just over an hour, but the whole time it felt like her heart had been in her throat. Her mouth was dry as she followed the new recruits from the ship into the landing bay. She stopped, silently noting the slight mustiness of the air, the recycled quality easily recognizable. Everything, including the oxygen, needed recycling in space.

All around her people swarmed, either around the ships or into the dogleg line that now formed ahead of her. Someone had opened the baggage locker of the shuttle, and the sound of dropping bags hitting the plascrete floor echoed in the air. Another crewmember guided trolleys to the other side of the shuttle, pulling out boxes with important day-to-day items for the ship, including vaccines and plants. She watched briefly, all the while listening to the alien cacophony. Voices called in welcome to old crewmembers, while new ones watched, many goggle-eyed in the fresh uniforms of newly minted officers and crewmembers.

Her gaze flicked around quickly, taking in the sights, sounds, and smells, pungent with oils and grease; burning smells from the scorched plascrete and the press of sweaty or nervous bodies. She joined the line silently, tacking onto the end, and stayed at parade rest, knowing the welcoming voice would cut through the air soon enough. She felt somehow disconnected from the main throng. Perhaps the knowledge that this was the outcome she had worked for years to achieve set her apart. However, still, she felt so...distant from everything around her. She smiled secretly at the bout of whimsy.

"Attention!" The voice boomed out over the plascrete of the docking bay, and she snapped her body into position, noting the commander who had bellowed the words. Technically, she outranked most members aboard the *Star of Ishtar*, except for the command and leadership staff, but she knew all newcomers had to join the welcoming parade, regardless of rank.

Fleet Captain Elphin came into view, his tired features topped by salt-and-pepper gray hair, which highlighted his cool blue eyes. Elara also recognized a body prone to a little middle-aged thickness.

Following behind him was his second-in-command, Duvall McCord. A young up-and-coming officer, his status as a fast-tracking officer heading toward his own command, with Elphin both his mentor and captain, had become almost legendary at the academy.

She looked closely at McCord, noting the dynamic drive of his actions and movements. Soon he would achieve a promotion to captain, and she rejoiced for her friend. She'd followed his career with interest and had to tamp down a smile as his eyes betrayed the shock of seeing her before settling into their flat command persona. So he hadn't been apprised of her deployment, she noted, and she had to restrain the tiny feeling of surprise and satisfaction. She filed that snippet of information away.

She caught sight of the man standing behind Duvall. Grayson Myatt. He'd made her heart beat faster for years. Tall and blond with a muscular build and a sexy, tight, little butt, he had pools of deep-blue eyes that had always made her think of forever. He had a growth of stubble on his chiseled jaw, and her fingers itched to touch his perfect lips. Yes, since the day he'd found her in that nasty ware-house tied down like a ragged animal, she'd worshipped him from afar.

Now she had her opportunity to tangle with him, hopefully much closer than any chance that had ever come her way before. With a sigh, she pulled her gaze back to the captain and forced herself to concentrate on his words. She couldn't afford to have her commanding officer angry due to her being distracted.

"Welcome to the *Star of Ishtar*. Most academy recruits want to join us because of what we represent, but on this ship, we only take the best of the best. So, if you made it here, you're the ones we wanted to take a look at. Getting here is only the first step. Staying here is harder to achieve. Our people are the best. Earn your place, and in return, we'll make you one of our crew—a member of the *Star of Ishtar*. Only the best and the brightest wear our uniform and badge. You'll be expected to perform to your absolute limit then give some more. We don't tolerate people who don't pull their weight. Do us proud and wear your uniform with pride." The captain looked out over the new members of his crew. His voice had echoed during his speech, and now it died away.

He scanned the faces before him, and she could almost read his thoughts. There were new security officers and a smattering of other crew. Some of them were young and impressionable, and she knew a few wouldn't make the cut as crewmembers. Others would carve out their place on the *Star of Ishtar* and move to better positions and placements, like she would: the new SurgiTech, a younger female, experienced but untried on board a ship. She smiled at that thought.

Some of those who stood with her would be replaced as they failed the exacting standards the captain set. She'd heard that he was a firm captain, fair but demanding. He'd have to be to command this ship. The Ishtar had well over five hundred at full capacity, and the captain could select their placements as his command staff saw fit from the many who applied to join the crew. She sensed his satisfaction with the choices in the relaxation of his body.

Abruptly, he turned to Duvall, breaking her study of him. "Get them to where they need to present themselves." His words echoed as he walked away. He had a purposeful stride. Quick but unhurried, like he knew where he was going and how to get there. A man who knew how to get what he wanted. Someone to respect and admire.

"My name is Commander Duvall McCord. I am your second-in-command, and my direct subordinate is Commander Grayson Myatt. While you are aboard the *Star of Ishtar* you will be required to fulfill your duties efficiently. As Captain Elphin said, do your job right and you will be one of ours, with all the benefits that come with being a crewmember of the *Star of Ishtar*."

He paused and eyeballed each of the newer recruits, those fresh from the academy. Many of them paled under his gaze, and she smiled inwardly. Even the older people in the line seemed to quake beneath his scowl. He'd always had that air of innate authority, even when barely out of the academy himself. She knew his methods and watched him make full use of the carefully practiced tone of presence.

"Each of you has been assigned. You will present yourselves to the chief of your section. Those details will be found in your orders. Commander Myatt has organized a team to escort you to your cabins. You will have approximately one hour to prepare. We've arranged for crewmembers to escort you to your superiors. Be ready to present for duty. Any issues, you will, of course, take up with your section commander. Should there be need to take any further action, you will see Commander Myatt. You should only see me if you are a command crewmember or as a point of discipline. I am not one for small talk, so if you present to me, have a very good reason."

He delivered the words slowly and deliberately, and Elara restrained a small smile on hearing at least one gulp from those in the line nearest her.

"We run a tight ship here. Discipline and commitment are the two key factors we look for beyond loyalty in our crew. You will from henceforth represent our ship everywhere, and we do not tolerate anything less than the best." He looked around once more, the stern demeanor he wore so well reinforcing the message. If she hadn't known him for so long, she too might have missed the hint of humor glinting in his eyes, the one many took for coldness.

Her legs ached, and she wanted to move and relieve the pressure on them, but she held herself still, waiting for the command to dismiss. She wouldn't let herself or him down now. Not after she'd worked so long to achieve this position.

As the new ST, she had no previous experience on ships. She had vast experience in the field, but Elara was aware that would count for little in the eyes of most of the crew. She didn't intend to signal a weakness to anyone and least of all on her first day aboard the *Star of Ishtar*. That thought held her still and controlled.

She had big shoes to fill after her predecessor, Jamieson, had retired, even though she knew she could fill the void he'd left behind. As a long-term member of the crew—over twenty years—his tenure on the *Star of Ishtar* had placed him aboard since its launch. Due to his experience in the heat of battle with the Ru'Edan he had made a name for himself as the coldest of cold in the hottest of situations.

She hoped to emulate that herself and carve out her own place aboard the Ishtar, as its crew lovingly knew her.

Duvall and Grayson knew how much she wanted to prove herself. They just wouldn't have expected it here, on the Ishtar.

She watched Duvall study her, then, quickly turning on his heel, call to those assembled, "Dismissed."

Once they started to move away, she softened her stance, preparing to turn when the call came.

"Sudonne! A moment if you please."

Elara turned to face Duvall. "Commander?"

"Welcome to the *Star of Ishtar*, Elara. While I am surprised you're the new ST, Grayson and I are pleased you could join us. But how did you manage to pull it off? Keeping it quiet that you were the new ST?" he asked, his voice deep enough to make most women shiver with anticipation.

She smiled, thinking it was a shame she didn't have any feelings for him except sisterly attachment, but then again, given his lack of deep commitment to women, maybe it wasn't such a shame after all.

She understood what drove him. He wanted his own ship and to captain his own future. They'd spent many nights over wine or ale discussing his beliefs that commitment grounded a person. Inwardly, she shrugged. He'd make those calls for himself, though she was sure that one day he would come across someone who would make him consider his choices a little more thoroughly.

"I'm pleased to be here, Duvall. Having an uncle who happens to be an admiral, he was able to let Captain Elphin know that I wanted to surprise you. It's a small world in the Admiralty. Elphin already knew of me, so he okayed my placement. Once the powers knew there was no impediments to me joining the crew, it was fairly simple from there." She felt a small smile creep onto her face, then let it drop away. "What do you think Grayson thinks?"

"Ah, still chasing him, are you?" He grinned, his eyes twinkling. "I think he'll be pleased you're finally old enough and you're here." He looked her straight in the eye. "But you may just need to remind him of that particular fact." He motioned for her to go before him, barking out a deep laugh. "Come on, I'll show you to your cabin."

Available from Love Books Publishing
Available in Ebook via Books2Read

Direct Autographed Copy
https://www.imogenenix.net/Warriors1

THE BLOOD BRIDE BY IMOGENE NIX

Hope just wants to be an ordinary nestling. She went to college and escaped, but now she's back and there's a secret everyone is keeping from her.

Xavier is the new master of the nest, ready to welcome home the daughter of the house who he has never met. He's unprepared for the woman who steals his breath and enchants him.

Now Hope and Xavier must fight for lives and those of the innocents. After all, it is only by overcoming the rogues that they will have a chance of a timeless future together. But will it be in time?

PROLOGUE

As silence descended on the house, the shadows grew—dark grays and blacks that bled into each other. First one figure then another broke away, making a run toward the house. Silent as the grave, they moved swiftly over dew-slicked grass. Then they stopped still. Waiting. Not a movement betrayed them until a signal propelled them back into action and they started crawling upwards. The walls damp coating no barrier to the intruders that ascended in the darkness.

The sound of each window breaking shattered the quiet—the figures were inside. Screams echoed through the night. Yet, in this area of large estates, heavy with noise-absorbing shrubbery, no one could hear those within. The blood-curdling screams went on and on before finally dying away.

Just one sound echoed through the night: The sobbing of a child.

The front door opened and figures trooped out—ghostly specters against an inky night sky, broken by a single outline. A child in white, carried at the center of the pack.

No sound broke the silence as they moved toward the trees surrounded the house.

Flames now licked at the manor: A deathly glow of oily smoke rising.

All that remained was a single person—wrapped in a cape of midnight blue beyond the house—watching them melt away.

Jemima moved toward the burning structure, breaking into a run as she breached the threshold. Vainly she attempted to enter, but the heat drove her back.

Now dashing tears from her face, she raced across the graveled driveway toward the gates, where the guardhouse was located. No sign of life existed within the building and some instinct of survival slowed her pace to a careful creep. Out of breath and heaving from exertion, she nervously checked within.

Small puffs of white vapor colored the glass. She darted from one window to another. Her cloak drawn tightly around her body, hoping it would camouflage her from sight.

Satisfied, Jemima entered through the heavy, wooden front door and moved toward the phone she spied on the floor. Her eyes darting here and there she dialed, listening to the rotary motor as it returned to the proper position. Time was short and if *they* came back, she needed to have shared the message.

The phone rang once. Twice. With a brrping sound it connected.

"Hello?" A male answered and she felt a warm flush of relief at the voice. A voice she knew well.

"The manor has been breached. The girl child taken." The words erupted and her hand trembled.

"On our way." The click of the receiver being replaced echoed loudly in the stillness of the room.

Copper. She smelled copper.

Her stomach soured, knowing it meant more deaths. Jemima looked around for the gun—a gun with deadly, holy water-infused copper bullets—she knew was hidden somewhere in the room. A gun she couldn't find. *No divine intervention exists here*, she thought.

Hopefully *they* didn't remain. Feeding. If they were still here, that's what they would be doing. She found a corner and scrunched down, hiding from sight.

Crouched low, she tried to stay as still as possible, listening for sounds of the vehicles she knew would be coming. She dug her fingers into the flesh of her arms; remaining aware enough to stop before drawing blood. That would surely bring them out. Jemima dragged the cloak around her to capture the warmth, yet there was little to be found.

The sounds of engines roused her from the corner of the room. Jemima inched toward the window, the lead of the old glass distorting her view, hearing raised voices she knew Mistress Cressida had arrived.

Jemima retreated. Remained hidden from the woman because if she knew, all may well be lost. From the shadowed room she listened to the conversation...

"It smells like Estersham." The Mistress' eyes closed. "If it is, we have a problem." She turned once more, her face set and eyes now glacial in intensity. "James?"

The man nodded as if he knew what was to come.

"If I take those steps, I cannot return. Another must stand in my place." Her voice hardened while her eyes glittered in the dim light, piercing in their intensity.

Then the Mistress' voice called out in the near silence. "You and yours have been my loyal servants for so many years. I took an oath to protect you long ago. I renewed it with marriage and births, over and over. Now, my home and yours have been breached and this child taken from us. The girl child, who will be the hope and salvation of our kind, was ripped from the bosom of our nest. I will repay your loyalty and I will get her back." The words of power rippled in the night and licked at Jemima's skin.

Available in Ebook
books2read.com/BloodBride-Nix

Direct Autographed Copy
https://bit.ly/TBB-Nix

ALSO BY IMOGENE NIX

Warriors of the Elector

- Star of Ishtar
- Starline
- Starfire
- Star of the Fleet
- Starburst
- The Star of Eternity

The Star of Ishtar & Starline - Print

Starfire & Star of the Fleet - Print

Starburst & The Star of Eternity - Print

Blood Secrets

- The Blood Bride
- The Illuminated Witch
- The Sorcerer's Touch

House Secrets (The Blood Secrets Continuation)

- As Dawn Breaks
- Immortal Consequences

The Automaton Series

- Haven House
- Nobel Crest

The Search Duology

- Miss Elspeth's Desire
- Miss Isabelle's Craving

Reunion Trilogy

- War's End
- The Assassin
- Executing Justice

The Reunion Trilogy in Paperback

Sex Love & Aliens

- Tangled Webs
- False Webs (Sex Love & Aliens Vol 1)
- Covert Webs (Sex Love & Aliens Vol 2)

21st Testing Protocol

- Cyborg: Redux
- Children Of A Greater Evil
- When Evil Came To Stay (Not Yet Released)
- Finis: The War To End All Wars (Not Yet Released)

Celtic Cupid Trilogy

- Blame The Wine
- A Stranger's Embrace
- Revenge On Cupid

The Celtic Cupid Trilogy in Paperback

Zombieology

- The Reset (2018 - Love At The End of The World)
- I Dream of Zombies
- The Six Million Dollar Zombie

<u>**Knights of Pleasure**</u>

- Silken Knights (Not Yet Released)

<u>**Single Titles**</u>

The Chocolate Affair (also in Print)

Falling In Love Again (Previously A Sapphire For Karina)

BioCybe (also in Print)

Hesparia's Tears (also in Print)

Tomorrow's Promise

A Bar In Paris (also in Print)

Inheritance Of The Blood (also in Print)

The Plan

Loving Memories (also in Print)

Hero of Heartbreak Hill (also in Print)

My One & Only

Curse Bound (coming 2021)

Raspberry Dreams (Not Yet Released)

<u>**Non Fiction**</u>

Self Publishing: Absolute Beginners Guide (With Suzi Love)

<u>**Written as Ciara Cave**</u>

25 Curated Ways To Get Rid Of Telemarketers

Book Signings for Absolute Beginners

ABOUT THE AUTHOR

Imogene is published in a range of romance genres including Paranormal, Science Fiction and Contemporary. She is mainly published in the UK and USA.

In 2010, Imogene Nix (the pen name not Imogene herself) was born. Imogene sat down and worked tirelessly for 3 months culminating in the book Starline, which became the first in a trilogy titled, "Warriors of the Elector." Since then she's had over 30 titles published and is now focusing on hybridising herself - with a mixture of traditionally published and self-published works.

In fact, she's taking control of many of her back catalogue books, which are slowly re-releasing as self-published titles.

Imogene is a member of a range of professional organisations world wide, and believes in the mantra of mentoring and paying it forward and is actively involved in mentorship (through NaNoWrimo and her vlog: In The Chair With Imogene Nix) and tutoring of new and upcoming authors.

In her spare time she loves to drink coffee, wine & eat chocolate and is parenting her spoiled dog and a ferocious cat along with her husband and 2 human daughters and looks forward to weekends away with her husband in their caravan "The Seven Year Hitch!" Do look forward to her caravan romance at some point!

To Contact Imogene

www.imogenenix.net
imogene@imogenenix.net

facebook.com/ImogeneNix

twitter.com/ImogeneNix

instagram.com/ImogeneNix

bookbub.com/authors/imogenenix